I became aware that Rhys Hiddwing was frowning at me. What could I have done to cause this response? I looked back at him, attentive, interested, but feeling a niggle of disquiet.

"We've met before," he said.

Hell, was my cover broken before I even began?

"I don't think so."

He tapped his fingers on the edge of the coffee table. "Yes, I believe we have. You see, I never forget a face."

LOOKING FOR NAIAD?

Buy our books at
www.naiadpress.com

or call our toll-free number
1-800-533-1973

or by fax (24 hours a day)
1-850-539-9731

Death Understood

A Denise Cleever
THRILLER

Claire McNab

THE NAIAD PRESS, INC.
2000

Printed in the United States of America on acid-free paper
First Edition

Editor: Lila Empson
Cover designer: Bonnie Liss (Phoenix Graphics)

Library of Congress Cataloging-in-Publication Data

McNab, Claire.
    Death understood : a Denise Cleever thriller / by Claire McNab.
        p.   cm.
    ISBN 1-56280-264-X (alk. paper)
    1. Women intelligence officers—Fiction.   2. Australia—Fiction.
3. Lesbians—Fiction.   I. Title.
PS3563.C3877 D43   2000
813'.54—dc21   00-030565

For Sheila

Acknowledgments

My deepest gratitude to Lila Empson, Sandi Stancil, and Judy Eda for editing, typesetting, and proofreading. Without their efforts, this book would not exist!

ABOUT THE AUTHOR

CLAIRE McNAB is the author of twelve Detective Inspector Carol Ashton mysteries: *Lessons in Murder, Fatal Reunion, Death Down Under, Cop Out, Dead Certain, Body Guard, Double Bluff, Inner Circle, Chain Letter, Past Due, Set Up,* and *Under Suspicion.* She has written two romances, *Under the Southern Cross* and *Silent Heart,* and has co-authored a self-help book, *The Loving Lesbian,* with Sharon Gedan. She is the author of two Denise Cleever thrillers, *Murder Undercover* and *Death Understood.*

In her native Australia Claire is known for her crime fiction, plays, children's novels and self-help books.

Now permanently resident in Los Angeles, she teaches fiction writing in the UCLA Extension Writers' Program. She makes it a point to return to Australia once a year to refresh her Aussie accent.

PROLOGUE

Although the sun was near the horizon, the heat rising off the red earth still shimmered the spiky outlines of the spinifex grass. The rocks of this ancient landscape, split by extremes of temperature and eroded by wind and occasional rain, lay tumbled and broken. Overhead a small flock of brilliant green budgerigars, chirruping, wheeled in dense formation, then plunged to settle on stunted trees.

Red-brown coats dusty, two dingoes, the female stretched in the shade of a twisted shrub, the male standing with ears pricked, watched the two humans prepare to break camp. The intruders had come into the wild dogs' territory during the night, walking steadily under the silver of a full moon. At dawn they'd set up a small tarpaulin near the narrow cleft that held the only permanent water hole in the area, and had rested under its shade from the heat of the day.

With half-grown pups to feed, the dingoes had circled the camp in the early light, slipping in and out of the meager cover, sniffing the scent of the food cooking. One human, seeing them, had snatched up a rifle. The sharp crack of the gunshot had sent them running, but they had returned with stealth to watch and wait.

The female dingo's ears twitched. Getting to her feet, she stared south at a plume of red dust, billowing like smoke. Soon the two humans heard the approaching roar of a vehicle. One clambered onto a large boulder and waved something white in wide circles. The other, hands on hips, yelled angry words.

The dogs shrank back as the noise grew louder. A truck, streaked with red dirt, bucked to a stop, its elongated shadow more substantial than any cover given by the scanty vegetation. The sudden silence swept like a balm over the desiccated land.

"What the hell are you doing here?"

A shot echoed and died in the cooling air. Then, after a while, the motor started again, and the vehicle, fat tires churning the dry dirt, made a wide circuit and went back the way it had come.

The sound had faded completely and a gentle evening breeze was blowing before the dingoes moved in to investigate. The body lay facedown, arms wide. The dogs waited, but there was no movement. Step by cautious step they approached until they could sniff the dark stain soaking the red earth around the head. The male pawed at an arm.

Made bold by the lack of response, the female dingo took a mouthful of shirt and, with one twist of her powerful neck, tore it away from the waiting flesh. She raised her head to give a short, sharp bark. It was time to call her pups to the kill.

CHAPTER ONE

The wide glass doors of the Hiddwing Institute hissed open, and a blast of cool air met the metallic heat of a Queensland summer day and my sweating face. A guard in a khaki uniform stationed just inside checked me over, but he clearly found my manner and demure blue dress acceptable, as he didn't challenge me.

I walked past him with a murmured hello. He gave an infinitesimal nod in acknowledgment, then went back to examining his nails. That was slack. If I had been intending harm, I would have chosen to look as inoffensive as possible — in fact, just exactly the way I did.

Before me stretched an expansive lobby, severe in black and gray. THE HIDDWING INSTITUTE appeared in huge silver letters on the wall facing me, the characteristic winglike appendage at the top of each upright stroke of the H looking even more ridiculous than usual. Below the name was a stylized representation of a burning torch, tilted at an angle as though an invisible hand were brandishing it.

The founders of the Institute, Oliver and Clara Hiddwing, had designed the logo themselves, and nothing had been changed since they had disappeared seven years ago. Underneath the name and torch appeared in red script the maxim they had adopted for the organization: *FROM THE PAST COMES THE FUTURE*. It was one of those sayings that sound significant, yet don't, when examined, make all that much sense.

I felt a thrill of excitement, balanced by a measure of anxiety. Months of patient preparation were paying off, presuming I didn't do anything dumb. My sensible heels clicked what I intended to be a self-assured counterpoint as I walked over dark gray tiles toward a tall, black reception desk.

There were two people behind the protection of the black marble. The young man, seated, had a narrow head set on a disconcertingly thick neck and shoulders. If I'd been him, I would've styled my hair to at least give the illusion that my skull matched my body, but his thin, black hair was slicked back. Bending over him, apparently giving instructions about something, was a cool blonde woman in a pale green tailored jacket.

An acrylic sign in front of the young man read JEFFREY. "Good morning, Jeffrey," I said, aiming for a cheerful, positive tone.

He gave me a look of professional welcome, but before he could speak, the woman straightened and blinked once at me. "And you are who?"

There was an almost indefinable accent, even in that short phrase. I knew it to be German — she had been born in Berlin thirty-three years ago. The photos I'd seen hadn't caught her aura of decisive power, but the pale hair, pale eyes, and definite jawline were all familiar.

"Denise. Denise Brandt." I said my name with confidence, as if it were really my own.

Her chilly expression immediately dissolved into a pleasant smile. "Excellent. You're early. We like that. I'll take you to Mr. Hiddwing's office immediately." She tapped Jeffrey sharply on the shoulder. "Have Elise join us there."

"She's not in yet."

"I see." An impatient click of her tongue conveyed her displeasure. "When she comes in, tell her I want to see her immediately."

As she moved from behind the reception desk, I could see that the rest of her lean body matched the taut line of her jaw. She extended her hand to give mine a brief, hard shake. "Ilka Britten," she said.

Of course I already knew that. In fact, I knew a great deal about Ilka Britten. Her real name was Vesta Schwatz, she spoke six languages well — three more than me. She'd been involved peripherally in four suspicious deaths, but there had never been any hard evidence to charge her with anything. She'd become an Australian citizen five years ago.

Ilka Britten looked supremely fit in a sinewy, no-nonsense way. Arms swinging, she walked off at a pace that had me almost trotting to keep up with her. I noted the green skirt of her suit was a decorous length, and that her shoes were flat. Her almost white hair was pulled back in a severe chignon. Her hair color was natural: mine a little less so. Normally dark blond, I'd had my hair expensively styled and streaked to fit my professional image.

Over her shoulder Ilka Britten said, "You've been in our Melbourne office for how long?"

"About six months."

Actually, it'd been more like four and a half, but I was anxious to establish my credentials as a reliable, dedicated member of the Hiddwing team.

"Mr. Radon spoke very highly of your contributions on the Frick matter. We have expectations that you will do even more valuable work here with us."

"I do hope so. I believe in everything that the Hiddwing Institute stands for, and I'd like to be part of the team."

Hearing the warmth of sincerity in my voice, I had a moment's worry that I was laying it on too thick, but Ilka was nodding her head, clearly pleased. "You will have every chance to fulfil that ambition, Denise. We are convinced you will not disappoint us. That is why we gave you the opportunity to join us here at the very nerve center of our organization."

Nerve center? For a moment I thought she might be making a sly joke, but a close look at her expression convinced me that it was highly unlikely that Ilka Britten had even a shadow of humor in her.

"It's an honor," I said, "to be at the nerve center."

At the end of the wide corridor was a heavy glass

door. Beside it on the wall a sign admonished: RESTRICTED ENTRY. UNACCOMPANIED VISITORS PLEASE RETURN IMMEDIATELY TO RECEPTION.

Ilka Britten punched a code into the keypad below the sign so rapidly that I only had time to catch the first three digits. The door slid open. "Don't delay," she said, "the door will close after eight seconds."

This was the inner sanctum, and had been furnished in generic luxury. The beige carpet was thick enough to turn an ankle, the filtered air was just a little too cool, the walls were papered with a discreet cream-and-pale-ocher pattern so inconspicuous that I had to look closely to see that it was made up of the Hiddwing name repeated over and over.

Portraits — not photographs, but oil paintings — were positioned to greet anyone who entered, each illuminated for optimum effect. Facing me was Oliver Hiddwing, his hard face serious, his grandly hooked nose looming over the slash of his thin-lipped mouth. The artist had given him rather more hair than I recalled from photographs I'd seen, and had colored it a pleasing chestnut, rather than the fading red it had been in reality. Beside Oliver Hiddwing his sister, Clara, lifted her heavy chin at the world. She was, I decided, even more formidable than her brother because there was intelligence in her painted eyes, and determination, rather than inflexible stubbornness, in the lines of her face.

Ilka had paused to let me admire the portraits. "Our founders," she said. "Without them, there would be no Hiddwing Institute."

I shook my head. "Unimaginable."

She looked at me, a faint frown creasing her forehead. I swore silently to myself. However tempting,

8

irony was to be avoided at all costs. I could hear my trainer snarling at me, *"Cut out the smart stuff, Denise. Your mouth will get you killed one day."*

With smooth haste, I went on, "What I mean is, the Institute has been a leader so long in the cultural and political life of the country that it's impossible to imagine Australia without that influence."

"Indeed." Ilka was nodding agreement. "And it is vital, absolutely vital, that we extend and deepen that influence." She took a deep breath, and I imagined her mounting an invisible soapbox. "The so-called progressive forces in society are determined to undermine everything that has made this nation a leader in the South Pacific."

This was tiresome. I had the irritated feeling that Ilka Britten, along with having no sense of humor, had an inexhaustible supply of set speeches that she would perform at any opportunity. Assuming what I trusted was an alert, keen expression, I said, "I *am* looking forward to meeting Mr. Hiddwing."

"Of course you are." She paused to lean into an open office door. "Will? Coffee et cetera, I think."

I didn't catch sight of Will, but a cheerful "Okay" came from within the room.

Ilka led the way down a broad, carpeted corridor, at the end of which was a polished wooden door. She ran her hand down a panel as though stroking an animal. "Rainforest wood," she said. "Very rare. Beautiful, isn't it?"

Thinking that it would be far more beautiful if such a scarce tree were still alive and growing, I said, "Everything is very nice here."

I repressed a grin. I was sounding trite and boring, and I was supposed to be a crash-hot PR operator. Ms.

Personality, with the ability to coax the most recalcitrant subject in the desired direction. I'd learned to cajole, to charm, to flatter, and, when necessary, to be tough. I liked the last mode best, but sadly found myself having to be super nice most of the time.

I tried a super-nice expression while Ilka rapped sharply on the door, paused, then opened it wide. Standing aside for me to go first, she announced, "Denise Brandt." She added approvingly, "She's a little early for her appointment with you, Mr. Hiddwing."

It was, of course, a huge office, dominated by a glass wall looking out into a tropical garden of riotous colors and luxuriant ferns. The furniture was cane, but not the tatty stuff that I remembered from my family home's sunroom — this was designer cane, lovingly made and finished in a light-colored satin sheen. The polished wooden floor gleamed, a gray slate step-fountain built into one wall made muted chuckling sounds as the water ran over semiprecious stones artfully arranged, and a vase of scarlet roses set on a cane stand scented the air.

The man in shirtsleeves who came from behind the desk, hand outstretched, had the same hooked nose as his father, but his mouth was fuller and his thick hair was a determined red. "Denise. I've heard wonderful things about your work for us. I'm so pleased to welcome you here."

He gestured toward a low table — cane, naturally — surrounded by four — more cane — chairs. "Ilka? Coffee, I think, and perhaps something to go with it?"

"Already ordered."

Rhys Hiddwing smiled, saying to me, "Ilka always has everything under control."

I smiled in turn — a moderate, pleasant smile. I took care to crinkle up my eyes a little. The Hiddwing Institute was very big on analysis of body language, and mine had to be just right. It was very important that I make a positive impression. Rhys Hiddwing had to learn to trust me, to begin to think of me as someone whose political and philosophical convictions marked me as one of the chosen, belonging in the company of those who thought of themselves as the keepers of the Hiddwing flame.

I went through the mental exercise that I'd been repeating to myself constantly during the last few days. I was Denise Brandt, only child of Phyllis and Robert Brandt, both deceased. I had been brought up by them with a reverence for traditional values. I could see, with the clarity and detail of a movie, the faces of my parents, and hear their voices as they imbued me with their ultraconservative, right-wing views. Phyllis and Robert Brandt were so vivid in my mind that for a moment it was hard to believe that they had never existed.

I became aware that Rhys Hiddwing was frowning at me. What could I have done to cause this response? I looked back at him, attentive, interested, but feeling a niggle of disquiet.

"We've met before," he said.

Hell, was my cover broken before I even began?

"I don't think so."

He tapped his fingers on the edge of the coffee table. "Yes, I believe we have. You see, I never forget a face."

CHAPTER TWO

Inwardly alarmed, but sounding faintly puzzled, I said, "If we'd met before, I'm sure I would have remembered you, Mr. Hiddwing."

He continued to regard me with narrowed eyes. Pinning down the time and place was obviously a challenge to him. I shuffled possibilities. Prior to this, we certainly hadn't moved in the same circles. Besides, from the time I'd volunteered for undercover assignments with ASIO — the Australian Security Intelligence Organization — strenuous efforts had been made to ensure that my likeness did not appear anywhere in the media. When, inevitably, I'd been called as a witness in prosecutions that had come from my undercover work, I'd been brought into the court through a back entrance, my evidence had been given in closed sessions, excluding the public, and I had only been referred to by an alphabetical letter, not even an assumed name.

And, in an effort to make sure that there was no one at the Hiddwing Institute who could recognize me, ASIO had run the name of every employee and scanned known financial and political supporters of the organization as well. Of course there was always the chance that someone could turn up out of the blue who knew me personally, but that was a risk that had to be taken.

"Perhaps it was a political function," I said, "or something like that."

The meetings Rhys Hiddwing would be likely to attend would be those where the participants were extreme far-righters, and therefore opposed to almost everything that I personally held dear. Normally I wouldn't have been seen dead in such gatherings, although in Melbourne, as part of my job with the Institute, I'd attended several and had conversed with fervor about traditional values and conservative beliefs.

Rhys Hiddwing cocked his head. "Maybe," he said. "I do travel a lot around the country, but I haven't been in Melbourne for some time."

Ilka was frowning at me as though I'd deliberately set out to cause a problem. "Have you been a participant at an HPV?" she demanded.

The acronym referred to Hiddwing Personal Values seminars, which were free and scheduled all over the country at regular intervals. Helped by a barrage of advertising, plus gifts of equipment to local schools and organizations, the seminars pulled in an amazing cross section of the general public, who were then entertained by a range of multimedia experiences. The seminars provided a reasonably subtle form of indoctrination — I called it brainwashing — and were the source of many new supporters.

I'd attended four HPVs as part of my preparation for this assignment, but regrettably Rhys Hiddwing had been at none of them. However, because I needed a fallback position, I said, "Yes, of course I've attended several seminars, but I don't recall seeing Mr. Hiddwing, although he may well have been there."

From Ilka's expression I gathered that she was astonished that anyone might be in her leader's presence and not be aware of that fact.

"Could it be," I said, "that it's the photo in my résumé you're remembering?"

He glanced over at the desk, where the open folder in front of his chair almost certainly detailed my entirely fictitious but impressive career highlights. The Hiddwing Institute had checked my employment record when I'd applied for the Melbourne position, but I wondered if he had been doing any follow-up inquiries now that I was moving up in the organization. It wasn't a matter for concern: The university degree I'd apparently completed was in the official records, and to avoid too close a personal check, many of the positions I was supposed to have held were overseas, or with huge companies where I'd be just a name in the personnel department files. The executives who had signed my references were either alerted to field any telephone queries or had recently left the company in question. It was a favorite ASIO ploy to select a person who had, for whatever reason, recently died, and use him or her as a reference, secure in the fact that there was no telephone link to the hereafter.

"It's possible," Hiddwing said, not sounding convinced. "I have been glancing over your réesumé, but I've got the feeling I saw you in person somewhere." He leaned back, smiling. "Won't worry about it now. I'm sure it'll come to me."

Even if he wasn't going to worry about it, *I* certainly was. This was a complication I hadn't anticipated, and it meant that I'd have to make contact with my control much sooner than I had intended.

"Coffee and the trimmings," said a light tenor voice from the doorway.

Ilka gestured for the young man to enter. "Thank you, Will. Put the tray on the coffee table."

"Will do." As he slid the laden tray onto the table, he gave me a small grin. "That's a joke," he explained. "I'm Will, and I will do."

Ilka pursed her lips, but Hiddwing said without rancor, "My son has a somewhat juvenile sense of humor."

Will Hiddwing had taken after his dead mother rather than his father. His light-framed body looked insubstantial next to Rhys Hiddwing's solid physique, there was no hint of red in his sandy hair, his nose had no suggestion of a hook to it, and his mouth was full and soft.

His father introduced us, and Will shook hands with me. "You're from Melbourne, right? Tansey was telling me all about you."

"Good, I hope," I murmured, secure that everything Tansey said was likely to be positive.

Will's smile widened. "For Tansey, surprisingly good."

Tansey Yates, a tiny woman with a large voice, ran the southern Hiddwing branch public relations with an iron hand. Once established there, I became her enthusiastic lieutenant, leaping to obey her commands, tactfully making suggestions that were effective — I'd had the advantage of prepping for the job with an international expert in PR — and generally making it clear that I admired her way of doing things. Since Tansey had previously gone through assistants like a hot knife through butter, she had warmed to me when I proved impervious to her rudeness, her unreasonable demands, and her tendency to blame her own mistakes on the nearest underling, whilst taking as much credit as possible for successes. Her vitriolic tirades were legendary, I found, but I endured those that came my way with stoicism.

One day I caught Tansey looking at me reflectively, and realized that the time to apply for a transfer was ripe. Mr. Radon, director of the Hiddwing Institute's southern branch, had not only noticed my achievements but had also praised me for my work, and Tansey Yates did not take kindly to competition.

Tansey hardly bothered to disguise her relief when I said that I wanted to apply for an opening that had come up at the head office — a position that had fallen vacant because the person in question had, with ASIO's covert intervention, been offered a PR job elsewhere so amazingly advantageous that he certainly could not turn it down.

Armed with a glowing recommendation from Tansey and Mr. Radon's enthusiastic endorsement, I was a sure bet for the new job, so I packed my things, said farewell to my colleagues, and flew to Brisbane. Part one had gone swimmingly; part two was going to be a great deal harder — and more dangerous.

It didn't, however, seem at all dangerous at the moment. Watched by Ilka, who was sitting upright, her hands folded in her lap, Will was pouring coffee from an elegant china pot into delicate, matching cups, and then handing around snowy linen table napkins to deal with the chocolate cake and apple tart.

Relaxed and faintly smiling, Hiddwing had swiveled in his cane chair so that he had one arm draped along the back of it. He was beautifully dressed: His white shirt was hand tailored, his muted blue tie was silk, his trousers had an impeccable crease, and his shoes were polished to a brilliant shine. He was wearing a heavy gold watch — Rolex, at a guess — and an elaborate signet ring that was engraved with the Hiddwing flaming torch.

He said to me, "You'll be working with Elise Gordon." He broke off to ask Ilka Britten, "Where is Elise? She should be here."

"Elise is late, as is common with her."

He grinned at her waspish tone. "Elise worked until eleven last night, preparing for the function, so I suppose she's entitled to a little extra time off."

"I also worked until after eleven."

"You're indispensable, Ilka, as always."

Mollified, she ducked her head. "Thank you."

Turning his attention to me, Hiddwing went on.

"There's an important function tonight at our estate. I do hope you'll be able to attend."

"Of course."

"Excellent. Will can give you the details. And you'll start work here tomorrow morning, pending a final clearance from Sid Warde."

"A final clearance?"

"Just a formality. As I'm sure you know, Sid's responsible for security in all our facilities, and he insists on the highest standards. This means that even though you were cleared to work in our Melbourne office, Sid is running a separate check before you get access codes and your ID badge for the Institute."

I added a couple of lumps of sugar to my coffee. Stirring it gently — my inclination is always to be too energetic — I said, "I've heard of Mr. Warde, of course, and I'm really looking forward to meeting him."

That wasn't altogether true. Of all the Hiddwing staff, Sid Warde was the one about whom I had the most apprehension. An expert on dirty tricks in political campaigns, he had a fearsome reputation as an enforcer who would do anything to destroy perceived enemies — and this destruction could include the physical, as he was a martial arts zealot.

Rhys Hiddwing had selected a fat slice of chocolate cake. "My weakness," he said indistinctly through a mouthful. After he'd swallowed, he dabbed at his mouth with his napkin and said, "I'm sure you'll like Sid. And now you're a member of our Institute family, you'll be on a first-name basis with everyone. You're to call me Rhys, for example."

Ilka clearly didn't support this we're-all-family informality. "That's all very well," she said, "but you know my thoughts on this." She paused, then began in lecturing tones, "Familiarity is not always the best route to take within an organization because —"

"I've heard it all before, Ilka." He made a dismissive gesture. "Forget it. Please."

She flushed, snapping her mouth shut and glaring around, apparently trying to find something or someone to blame for her embarrassment. "Will? Have you got Denise's security package ready?"

"Almost. You asked me to get the coffee, so I had to stop and do that."

His airy reply gave her the opportunity she was looking for. "*Almost* isn't good enough. How often have I said to you, 'Do it immediately, do it right, and check, check, check to make sure you've accomplished your task'?"

Will's expression showed that I wasn't the only one who found Ilka wearisome. "Right," he said without enthusiasm. He quirked an eyebrow at me. "Want to come along to my lair? I promise you'll be safe with me."

Ilka's top lip lifted in a quickly repressed sneer. My background briefings hadn't indicated any antipathy between Hiddwing's son and Ilka, so perhaps the muted conflict between them was of recent origin.

Rhys got to his feet and stretched expansively. "I'll send Denise along in a few moments, Will. Right now I'd like a few private words with her." His glance included Ilka, whose mouth tightened. When she went to clear the coffee table, he said, "No, leave that. I'll be having another cup."

When we were alone, he settled himself back in the chair with a sigh. "Personalities," he said. Spreading his hands, he went on, "I'm sure, being in

PR, you know how it is. People tend to see just their own little corner of the action. Not the big picture." He leaned forward. "Can you see the big picture, Denise?"

Was this some kind of test? Okay, I'd go for it. "I can," I said.

He nodded slowly. "Indeed? And what's the big picture you see as far as the Hiddwing Institute is concerned?"

"No less than the transformation of Australian society."

He gave a half-laugh. "You surprise me."

I looked modest.

Growing serious, he said, "My sister and I have great plans for the Institute and its role in restoring the values that have been shredded by what radicals call *social progress*." These last two words were said with deep scorn.

I had no intention of interrupting, but he still put up a hand, as if to stop a comment. "I know what you're thinking. Not all progress is wrong, and I agree. I fully support the equality of women, for example."

In fact, this had been a long standing commitment of the Hiddwings. Both his aunt, Clara, and his father, Oliver, had been firm supporters of women's rights — that is, if the women concerned were of a certain racial and societal group. The literature that the Institute churned out from its own publishing company — which went under the odd name of Prophet's Calling — had always included the theme of equal opportunity for the sexes, and Rhys had a sister who embodied feminism, albeit with a conservative cast.

He was watching me closely. "I believe we'll work

well together, Denise. You have the skills, the experience, and, I believe, you may well share the Hiddwing tenets. I'll be watching your progress with interest."

"Thank you, Mr. Hiddwing."

"Rhys, please."

"Rhys."

He uncoiled himself from the chair with an ease that contradicted his heavy build. "I'll see you tonight, then."

After making the right noises, I closed his office door behind me and made my way down the hall to Will's room. Ilka had disappeared, and the soft hum of the air conditioning and a distant burst of laughter was all that could be heard. I had a sudden cold feeling that they were on to me, and that I was trapped, so that when I tried to leave this shrine to die-hard conservatism, I wouldn't be able to get the glass security door to open.

"Hey," said Will from behind me. He'd approached soundlessly on the thick carpet. He pointed into his little office. "Want to sit down, or have you things to do?"

"I've got to do something about finding accommodations. I'm staying in a hotel at the moment."

"Ask Jeffrey at the front desk. He's always looking for people to share the house he rents."

"Always?" I said. "That's not very encouraging."

Will laughed. "He's not Jeffrey the Ripper, if that's what you're worrying about." He shoved a red plastic folder into my hand. "Here's all the stuff about the building. Entries, security measures — all that stuff. I'll give you a temporary entry card to get you past the car park security tomorrow morning. And I've got a numerical password for you to learn for entry into the offices. I'm not supposed to give it to you until Sid does a final check, but to hell with it." He grinned at me. "You look trustworthy to me. Now, come with me, and I'll show you the ropes."

When we reached the glass door I'd fantasized not opening for me, Will said, "For security reasons these executive offices are entirely separate from the rest of the building, and only selected personnel have key codes to get in."

"I don't imagine I'm selected personnel."

He grinned sideways at me. "Not yet, Denise, but I have high hopes for you."

I had to give credit to Will Hiddwing. In a few efficient minutes he had covered the essentials about the operation of the Institute building, taken me on a rapid tour of the three floors of offices and meeting rooms, had indicated where I'd be working, had taken a Polaroid photo for my ID card, and, after ascertaining that neither Elise Gordon nor Sid Warde was available, had deposited me back in the lobby. "See you tonight. Jeffrey will give you instructions on how to get to the estate."

The lobby was empty except for the security guy at the front. Behind the black reception desk I could see Jeffrey's bent head. So intent was he on his reading that he jumped when I spoke. "Hi. Remember me? Denise Brandt."

He grinned at me. "Of course. The new PR person."

I peered over the counter at the book he was reading. "Something interesting?"

His smile disappeared, to be replaced by a grave

expression. "Do you know how to perform a tracheotomy?"

He didn't seem to be joking. "I'm a bit rusty with tracheotomies," I said.

"It could happen any time. An emergency, and you're the only one who can save a life." He fumbled in his pocket and came up with a folded pocketknife. "Razor sharp," he said, flicking out a shiny blade. "And a ballpoint, you need a ballpoint pen."

I made an encouraging noise, but he hardly needed urging. "Right, here's the sitch. The Heimlich maneuver's failed, and your victim's turning blue. No coughing, no gasping, no nothing." He frowned at me. "Well?"

"I'm guessing an obstruction."

His satisfied nod showed this was the answer he wanted. "On the floor with the victim, head back, throat exposed. Then here" — he tapped at his neck below his prominent Adam's apple — "cut here, between here and the cartilage below. Just a slit. Got that?"

"Got it — but *erk!*"

"Then you take the ballpoint — without the ink bit, of course — and ram the tube into the throat. The victim can now breathe."

"Gosh," I said.

Jeffrey shoved back from the desk and stood, revealing that he was considerably taller than I'd thought. He seemed to have devoted a great deal of time to bodybuilding, having the barrel chest and meaty shoulders of someone dedicated to working out. His thick neck made his narrow head look all the more incongruous.

"How are you with first aid?" he asked.

As part of my training I'd done advanced medical courses, including the instructions given to paramedics in battle situations, but I wasn't about to boast about that here. "First aid?" I said. "I really don't know much about it. Hate the sight of blood." Realistic shudder. "And injections . . . well, I just faint."

I managed to stop myself from further embroidery. I'd had pointed out to me countless times that it was a serious weakness in an undercover agent to get so carried away that the story one was telling collapsed from weight of detail.

"Actually, I'm quite an expert with emergencies," said Jeffrey. "For instance, do you know what to do if a tsunami strikes?" He beamed at me. "*I* do."

He paused to let that sink in, then added, "And snakebite. I'm crash-hot at snakebite."

"Will said to ask you for the address of the estate," I said, although I knew exactly where it was, and was familiar with aerial views, architect's drawings, and the topography of the local area. Denise Brandt could know none of these things, so I bent over the printed sheet he fished out from behind the desk and frowned over the detailed map and his rather muddled directions.

"How long will it take? I'm staying at the Windsor Hotel."

"About forty minutes, tops."

I creased my forehead and pursed my lips in an anxious-to-do-the-right-thing manner. "And I forgot to ask anyone what to wear. I mean, do I have to get dressed up?"

He raised his heavily-muscled shoulders in a shrug.

"Just sort of good casual, I suppose. There'll be a barbie, and all that stuff. And quite a few VIPs."

"Oh? Anyone I'd know?"

"Helena Court-Howerd. I bet you've heard of her."

I had indeed, and not only in the media, where she was was often featured. ASIO had an extensive file on Helena Court-Howerd, widow of a self-made multi-millionaire and generous supporter of the Hiddwing Institute. Not quite so openly she promoted the political careers of like-thinking candidates who would — and did — do her bidding when elected.

"Of course I've heard of her," I said with a measure of indignation. "You forget — I *am* in PR."

CHAPTER THREE

The security guard stepped in front of me just as I reached the front doors of the building. "Stop right there," he said.

My heart put in a few unplanned beats. "Pardon?"

"Are you Denise Brandt?"

I glanced over my shoulder, then back at the guard. He had a stolid, plodding quality about him, and his navy uniform was one size too small. Close inspection of his upper lip indicated that he was attempting to grow a mustache. "Well," he said, "are you?"

Maybe they were playing cat and mouse with me, letting me get almost to safety before seizing me. I read myself a quick mental lecture about letting my imagination, always lurid, run away with me. Even after this instant pep talk, I measured the distance to the door. A quick chop to this guy's throat and I'd be out and free in the summer sun.

Get a grip, Denise.

"I'm Denise Brandt."

He tapped the pager clipped to his belt. "They told me to tell you to wait. So I'm telling you."

"Who did?"

He made a vague sweeping gesture toward the back of the lobby. "They did." He looked at me impassively, then his face was split with a sudden smile that showed a set of excellent teeth. "Actually it was I. B., the boss lady of the outfit. I always do exactly what she says. I don't want to lose my head . . ." He paused, then glanced down at the front of his pants. "Or worse."

I had to smile. "Ilka Britten, I suppose you mean."

"She's one tough lady. Terrifies me, I don't mind telling you."

His droll tone made me rapidly revise my original opinion of him. "You know I'm Denise," I said. "What's your name?"

"Kevin, but you can call me Kev."

Before I could say anything more, a woman came dashing across the lobby, calling out in a breathless contralto, "Denise! You're Denise, aren't you? Thank God Kevin stopped you. Ilka said you might still be here. Just got in. Parked in the underground garage, came upstairs and she told me. Should have been here. Late night. My apologies."

"You're Elise."

"Oh yes! Elise Gordon." She slapped the side of her face. "Sorry, should have introduced myself right away." Her shoulder bag fell to the floor as she put out her hand to shake mine. "Oops! I'm bloody clumsy. Anyone tell you that already?" She gave a hoot of laughter. "Christ knows how much data I've lost by pushing the wrong computer key."

I gave her the once-over as I helped her gather the things that had spilled out of her bag. Floral sundress, absurdly high backless sandals, several silver bangles clinking on her wrist. She had masses of curly chestnut hair and a pretty, high-colored face that didn't show her true age. I knew she was almost forty, but she looked ten years younger.

Tossing the last makeup item — she seemed to have a beauty shop's worth — into her bag, along with a bulging wallet and assorted electronic devices, she said, "Come back to Jeffrey's desk. You can tell me where you staying."

"Where I'm staying? I'm in a hotel at the moment."

Elise was already walking off. "Come on," she called. "You're going to the thing tonight, aren't you? You should. In fact, you must."

"Actually, I am."

She reached the reception desk and swung around to face me. "Great. I'll drive you. Least I can do, under the circumstances."

The possibility she drove the way she talked was quelling. I said hastily, "Jeffrey gave me a map and full instructions. I'm sure I can find it."

"You've already got a car?"

"I rented one at the airport."

A look of scorn crossed her face. "Rented? That'll be some mundane, boring sedan. You'll be better off with me. Got an MGB, entirely redone. British racing green. Cost me a fortune, I can tell you, but turns heads everywhere I go."

Jeffrey, grinning, said, "The MG will be more exciting, but if you want safety first, you'll let *me* drive you."

Elise frowned as Jeffrey warmed to the idea.

"Why don't you come with me?" he said. "I've done defensive driving courses, and I'm certified in all adverse conditions, including flood, fire, and snow. And terrorist attack. Bet you don't know what to do in a terrorist attack."

"Scream a lot?"

He shook his head. "Not likely to help. In fact, could be counterproductive."

"Jeffrey always expects the worst," said Elise. "He's taken being prepared to the most ridiculous extremes."

He didn't seem at all put out by her derisive tone. "I'm not a pessimist," he said, "but a realist. Things happen, and I'm going to be the one who's ready for them."

Elise was checking her watch. "Gotta go. Thanks, Jeffrey. You'll drive Denise then? Don't be late."

I watched her hurry off toward the lifts. "And I thought she was keen to show me her MG," I said.

With a sly smile, Jeffrey said, "Elise likes to offer to do things, but she's not so good at following through. You'll get used to her after a while. Don't take her too seriously, and you'll be okay."

I nodded, a little uncertain. "It's all so new," I said with a touch of pathos.

Jeffrey didn't notice. "Pick you up at six-thirty, okay? The Windsor Hotel, you said?"

"I'll be out front. And I'll bring my map."

He frowned. "You won't need it. I know where we're going."

"I'll have it as a backup, in case you toss me out of the car at some point." When he blinked at me, I added, "After all, *you're* the one who believes in being prepared."

Jeffrey gave a snort of laughter. "I can see you're going to liven things up around here," he said in a tone of deep approval.

On the way out of the building I exchanged a few pleasantries with Kev. Cultivating a friendly relationship with security staff was calculated — the possibility always existed that I might need to have the rules bent for me in the future. In this case it wasn't a chore, because Kev had a dry wit that sent me chuckling out into the hot day.

I glanced back at the bland facade of the Institute. Its clean lines made it look like any other small, modern office building, but inside its innocuous exterior forces were at work that threatened my country's security.

ASIO had long suspected the Hiddwing Institute of perverting the political process at both state and federal levels throughout Australia, not only by vote-stacking in party selection processes, but also in the use of phantom voters, who existed on the electoral rolls but not in reality. And there were disturbing incidents that could be indirectly traced back to the Institute — a firebombing, several beatings, and two mysterious deaths, one a campaign worker for an outspoken opponent of the Hiddwings, and another a politician whose ethnic background was Indian.

Recent rumors of darker and more far-reaching plans, plus the announcement that Rhys and Becky Hiddwing were taking legal action to have their missing father and aunt declared officially dead, thus freeing up millions of dollars of inheritance, had moved the ASIO investigation into high gear and put me undercover into the Institute.

I'd parked in the street in the shade, but this had disappeared by the time I got back to the car. The hot air hit my face as I opened the driver's door. I slid in gingerly, burned my hands on the steering wheel, and turned the fan on high. Joining the stream of traffic, I thought ruefully that I was in the hot seat more ways than one.

Back in the chilly embrace of my hotel room — I'd left the air conditioning on high — I contemplated my options. I couldn't imagine where Rhys Hiddwing had seen me before, but he seemed convinced he had, so it was a problem that had to be dealt with. He didn't seem to be the type to let it drop, so the best thing to do was to provide him with the time and place in the past where he could have conceivably caught sight of me.

He'd been under ASIO surveillance for some time, so his movements around the country were documented. I recalled that I'd looked at a breakdown, but couldn't remember much, except that he'd given many very well-received speeches to various conservative groups, and that before the last elections he had been an honored guest at right-wing politicians' rallies.

My control, Myra, would have to be told the news. She wouldn't be happy, but unlike my trainer, who was apt to criticize me without mercy, Myra was always supportive. Sometimes I wondered what she really thought of me, but evidently she had made it a personal rule that nothing but strictly work issues would ever be discussed, as any attempt of mine to gently probe had been smoothly parried.

I didn't know much about her, except that her career with ASIO had been a very successful one. Myra wasn't really Myra — I happened to know her real name was Cynthia — because her name was changed for each new mission. For security reasons I'd never have this confirmed, but it was likely that she was simultaneously the liaison officer for several other agents in the field.

Names had always fascinated me, particularly in the cases where one so obviously didn't suit the person concerned. I'd known Bruces who should have been Stevens, and Debbies who should have been Rachels. Myra definitely didn't suit her, and she didn't really seem to be a Cynthia either.

I'd decided Myra didn't have a good ear for names. She'd tried to saddle me with Diana for this mission, pointing out that I could keep my first initial, but I dug my heels in and insisted that I stay Denise, the same as I had before in two other undercover assignments. She had very reluctantly agreed, so I had become Denise Brandt.

I pictured Myra in my mind's eye. She was attractive in an idiosyncratic way. Not strictly pretty, she had a mobile, expressive face and short, spiky hair.

Her lanky body was all angles, but she managed somehow to always seem graceful, whatever odd position she assumed. Myra was inclined to fold herself into chairs, inhabiting the furniture rather than merely sitting in it. It was hard to explain, but she was one of those people who made an indelible mark on one's consciousness, lingering there like a silent exclamation.

I'd often wondered about her. She knew my sexual orientation, as she had access to my records. ASIO was perfectly happy to employ individuals who were straight, gay, or bi, as long as each person was open and out, so that blackmail about sexual preferences could never be an issue. Intrigued, I'd used the usually reliable office telegraph to make a few oblique inquiries about Myra, but to my chagrin, had got nowhere.

I picked up my bag and slung it over my shoulder, wishing it had the weight of a firearm in it. This showed a touch of paranoia, as it was highly unlikely that I was under even cursory surveillance. Nevertheless, I had to act as though I were, so instead of using the telephone in the cool comfort of my hotel room, I found myself going down to the hotel lobby, purchasing a phone card in the gift shop, and then launching myself into the heat and glare of the afternoon.

Brisbane had always been one of my favorite cities: Smaller than Sydney and Melbourne, and somehow friendlier and more relaxed, it was set on a lazy river. Its warm, subtropical climate filled its parks and reserves with gorgeous flowers and shrubs. On previous visits I'd spent time walking in the splendid Botanic Gardens and had cruised around the little islands of Morton Bay, where the Brisbane River emptied into the sea, but I had no time for such pleasant diversions this time.

The nearby shopping mall was crowded with people who all seemed to have nothing to do this Monday but stroll along, all the while talking at the top of their voices. I joined the throng, automatically checking for security, and noting several cameras trained on the concourse and two security guards patrolling.

Half the visitors to the mall seemed to be eating ice cream, and I was swept with a sudden desire to taste some myself. I found an ice-cream bar doing great business, waited in line while assorted kids accompanied by impatient parents lingered over which flavors to select, and finally got served a double cone — one scoop of rum-and-raisin and one of a rather startling pink watermelon.

It wasn't an ideal combination, I found, but I devoured it anyway, luxuriating in the cold, sweet texture as it slid down my throat. A sudden stab of guilt that I was enjoying myself when I was supposed to be working sent me looking for a public telephone. There was a bank of them by the rest rooms, which had a stream of people barging in and out, so I chose the telephone on the quietest end, hard up against the window of the Curl Up & Dye hairdressing salon.

The salon seemed trendy, being full of clashing colors and blown-up pictures of individuals I recognized as being up-and-coming music and screen personalities. A row of clients sat in chairs while a flock of preternaturally thin young women and one young man ministered to their heads. Blaring music made any communication inside the salon seem problematic, but that level of background noise was what I was looking for, as it would make a telephone conversation almost impossible to record, even with a sensitive directional microphone.

A quick check of the hairdressing salon didn't indicate any interest in my direction, and no one using the rest room facilities paid me the slightest attention. There was a suspicious-looking man two telephones along from me, but he looked more like a leering, down-at-the-heels pervert than anything else. I couldn't hear what he was saying, but from the reaction of the young girls who walked by him, his comments were more than unwelcome.

My low opinion of this guy was obviously shared by the mall security team, as the two officers I'd seen earlier descended on him and, despite his spluttering indignation, swept him away between them.

Being careful to position my body so that it would be impossible for anyone to read the sequence, I punched in the first of the list of numbers I'd memorized. The phone rang nineteen times, enough to discourage most wrong numbers, then a beep indicated the computer was waiting for my identifying code.

"Is this really necessary?" I said to the receiver. It beeped again in a bored fashion.

I put in five numbers, waited ten seconds, then put in five more. There was a twenty-second delay, then Myra said, "Yes?"

"It's me."

"I know that. I'm just wondering *why* it's you." She sounded somewhat amused. "Is there a problem?"

"Could be. Kookaburra thinks he's seen me before."

I found myself smirking at the idea of Rhys Hiddwing being a Kookaburra, considering the bird's manic chuckle. Inspired by the "wing" in Hiddwing, it had been Myra's bright idea to give the main players at the Institute avian names for security purposes. I'd suggested Fairy Wren for Rhys Hiddwing, just to see what Myra would say, but she'd replied that she was happy with her choices: Kookaburra for Rhys; Rosella for his sister, Becky; Shrike for Ilka Britten; Goshawk for Elise Gordon; Hummingbird for Sid Warde.

The image of the dangerous Sid Warde as a tiny hummingbird, its wings a blur as it hovered to suck nectar from a blossom, was comical. It was meant to be: Myra knew very well that I was worried about the man, and she wanted to defuse him to some extent by giving him a ludicrous code name.

"How serious is it, Denise? Enough to pull you out?"

"I think we can get around it." As briefly as possible I explained what had happened at the meeting and what I proposed as a solution. I told her my movements for the rest of the day, including my visit to the Hiddwing Estate that evening.

"Have a good time," she said with a soft chuckle. "And don't drink too much."

She promised to get back to me, and rang off. For a moment I felt as though a lifeline had been severed, but with a mental shake I stopped being Agent Denise Cleever, and became Denise Brandt again, an enthusiastic employee of the prestigious Hiddwing Institute who had to find accommodations somewhere not too far from my new workplace.

By late afternoon it was clear I was going to have to spend more time than I'd bargained for to find anything appropriate. I'd gone to the agency whose ad in the yellow pages had promised "Fast, personal service! Accompanied inspections! Your new home is our obsession!"

This last statement had proved to be not entirely accurate. I'd been shown several flats, none of which was acceptable. "I'm a bit worried about security," I'd said to the apathetic young woman who was showing me around the rental properties.

"Oh yeah?" she said, not a bit interested. From her manner it was clear she didn't envisage a long-term career in the area of matching accommodations with nitpicking would-be renters.

And I was a little more nitpicking than most. I didn't want a place that had fences or shrubbery too close to the building; I wanted solid entry doors, although the locks weren't important as I intended installing my own interior/exterior deadlocks; I needed at least two escape routes from the apartment; I was looking for vehicle parking that was well lit and preferably behind security gates.

"Sorry," she said after several hours of traipsing in and out of buildings, "but we just don't seem to have what you want, do we?"

"Appears that way."

"Well then . . ."

"I'll be back tomorrow," I said. "After work."

"Oh? I won't be there." There was no regret in her voice. "You'll have to see Mr. Plover."

"Mr. Plover?" I grinned, thinking of the Hiddwing code names. "There are birds twittering around everywhere."

She looked at me narrowly, and I remembered, too late, that her name was Kerry Byrd.

CHAPTER FOUR

Jeffrey was right on time, and driving, I was repelled to see, a rather elderly but beautifully maintained beige-colored Volvo, complete with additional bull-bars front and back, and heavy roof-racks, perhaps meant to add protection in a rollover.

I despised beige as a color, and Volvos had never gained my affection — in fact, I actively disliked them. This explained why my expression, which I'd intended to indicate mild anticipation, had changed. As I climbed into the passenger seat Jeffrey said, "What's wrong? Your mouth's all twisted up one side."

"I'm sneering."

"At me?" he said, affronted.

The inside of the Volvo showed the same tender loving care as the exterior, so I could hardly tell him that the object of my derision was his beige vehicle. "Just a general sneer, not aimed at anything in particular."

He looked at me sideways. "Right," he said. He looked me over. "Nice outfit."

"Thanks." I thought the matching pale blue silk pants and top were pretty nice myself.

After watching me do up my seat belt, Jeffrey leaned over to check that it was securely fastened. Then it was time to push down the indicator, place his hands carefully at the ten-to-two position on the steering wheel, and check all the mirrors. After taking the extra precaution of swiveling his head around to make sure the way was clear, he pulled out from the curb.

I'd resigned myself to puttering along in the slow lane, possibly with one indicator blinking infuriatingly to indicate a turn never taken, but Jeffrey proved to be a smooth, efficient driver who went with the flow of the traffic, aware both of the vehicles around him and also what was happening some way ahead.

As we left the city behind the traffic thinned. The Hiddwing estate was situated in the heavily rain-forested foothills to the west of Brisbane. I'd visited the area when staying with distant relatives years ago and remembered it as unspoiled bushland, full of beautiful picnic places and challenging bush-walking trails.

I glanced over at Jeffrey. His attention was concentrated ahead, and I had the opportunity to look at him closely. My detailed briefings had included only key members of the Institute's staff, so I knew nothing about Jeffrey except for his name. I put him in his late twenties, although it was possible he was younger. He had an undistinguished face, with a short nose and a nondescript chin, but his neck was a thick column, and the overdeveloped muscles of his shoulders swelled under his deep blue sports shirt. He'd devoted time to his thighs too, as they strained the seams of his tan slacks. He would walk, I was sure, with that almost-waddle that most dedicated bodybuilders were forced to use.

"You work out?" I said.

"Every second day." He shot me a quick smile. "Got tired of having sand kicked in my face, and all that, so I decided to do something about it. No one says boo to me now."

"I don't imagine they do."

He took a hand off the wheel to bend his elbow, clench his fist, and thereby create an extremely impressive biceps bulge. "And brute strength's a help on the staff retreats."

The Hiddwing Institute used compulsory wilderness camping trips as a means of bonding employees, and I'd spent two weekends at various places near Melbourne trekking through heavy undergrowth and trying to look as though I was having a good time. I did enjoy the landscape — what I found trying was the company of those in the group who complained incessantly. The most vociferous of these was my boss, Tansey Yates, who was bitter because even her impressive influence in management couldn't get her out of these compulsory excursions, and she was going to make sure everyone knew in exhaustive detail exactly what she thought about it.

I said with moderate enthusiasm, "The Melbourne office had staff weekends every couple of months."

Jeffrey made a dismissive noise. "Nothing like the ones you'll get up here."

"No?"

"These are fair dinkum tests of endurance, not a day at the beach. Stretch you to the limit. And everyone at the Institute's expected to attend at least four a year. And at least one of those is something *really* challenging, like the Kimberleys or Cape York."

Playing the part of new employee, I said, "Do the Hiddwings go too?"

"They're the keenest of the lot. That is, except for Will. He's always looking for some excuse to get out of it."

There was enough scorn in his voice to be interesting, so I said, "Will's very nice, but he doesn't seem the outdoor sort."

Jeffrey compressed his lips in the manner of one who wanted to say something, but thought better of it. It was worth pursuing, so I said, "I suppose one day Will expects to take over the Institute from his father."

"No way!"

"No?"

Jeffrey glared through the windscreen at the road ahead. "Long term, I don't think Will Hiddwing is all that interested."

I waited for him to go on, but instead he gave me a quick, assessing glance, and, in an obvious move to change the subject, said, "You look pretty fit, Denise,

41

but out in the bush that doesn't count for anything if you're not prepared for every eventuality, and I don't suppose you are."

I looked appropriately concerned. "Well, I do aerobics classes, but I suppose that's not enough."

"Not nearly enough."

In truth, I was prepared for most eventualities. I wondered how Jeffrey would respond if I told him that I'd been trained in unarmed combat, and, when dire circumstances had forced me to, I had killed.

"It's funny they'd still be so keen on this sort of wilderness thing," I said, "especially when you consider what happened to Clara and Oliver Hiddwing."

"No one knows what happened to them."

"That's my point, isn't it? They were off on some outback trek or whatever in the middle of nowhere and they disappeared. These hikes can be dangerous."

He released his two-handed grip on the wheel for a moment to reach over and pat my hand in a big-brotherly sort of way. "It's natural to be worried, Denise, but I'll keep an eye on you when we're at the next retreat."

His face was flooded with sudden enthusiasm. "Actually, the next one's scheduled for next month in virgin rain forest, and it's going to be tough. If you like, I can work out a training regimen for you, so you won't embarrass yourself. What do you say?"

"Gee, I'm not that keen. Like, I don't want to build up big muscles. They look great on *you*, but . . ."

This brought a chuckle from Jeffrey. "You don't know the first thing about it, do you?" he said indulgently. "I'll design a program for you that I guarantee won't bulk you up."

"I'll think about it."

There was a mini-traffic jam ahead of us, and we joined a long line of vehicles slowed to walking pace. When we got to the source of the trouble, it proved to be a relatively minor rear-end collision. "Tsk," said Jeffrey, "inattentive driving — that's what causes most accidents."

We edged past the interlocked vehicles and the two irate drivers waving their hands around as they each accused the other of causing the collision. Jeffrey shook his head. "Look at the body damage on those cars. Never happen to a Volvo."

I steeled myself to the Volvo-owners' instructional talk. I was well aware that this brand of vehicle was supposed to offer superior protection in the event of a crash. My much older brother, Martin, had had a succession of dark-toned Volvos, and I could still hear his standard, irritating lecture about how they were the safest car on the road.

Naturally, the first car I bought was bright red and fast and decidedly not a Volvo. "Typical," Martin had said in the critical tone he was accustomed to using with me. As a kid sister I had been a disappointment to him — he had obviously hoped for someone more malleable, more inclined to view her elder brother with awe and respect. Instead he got me.

We'd grown even further apart over the years, and now I did my best to avoid ever thinking about Martin at all, but for some reason Jeffrey's blasted Volvo had brought it all back. To banish my brother to the back of my mind where he belonged, and to forestall any comments on the Volvo safety record that Jeffrey might be about to deliver, I said, "How long have you been at the Institute?"

"A couple of years." He paused, then went on, "I

suppose you're thinking it's not much of a job, being on the reception desk."

"I wasn't thinking that at all."

"Because I'm not going to be staying on the desk much longer. I'm training to lead a booster brigade."

"Really?" I was pleased with the note of admiration I'd injected into my voice, particularly as I'd observed the operation of booster brigades in Melbourne and thought the whole concept odious. The name was misleadingly innocuous: The members of the group, usually young and fit, infiltrated meetings and conferences held by organizations espousing views contrary to the Institute's. "Boosts," as they called themselves, had extensive training in techniques to disrupt the proceedings and to intimidate anyone who put up any opposition.

Jeffrey had taken my approval for granted. "Being a boost is what I've been aiming for, and, though I know it's a cliché, it's true — the ends do justify the means. I support everything that the Hiddwings stand for." He turned his head to look at me. "Don't you?"

"Yes, of course."

I didn't sound fervent enough. He frowned, and went on, "You've got to really be convinced, Denise." His voice had the certitude of a true believer. "No lip service. No halfhearted endorsement. We're fighting a war, here, undeclared, but still a war, and what's at stake is the future of Australia."

I murmured an affirmative reply, repressing a pang of regret that Jeffrey, whom I was starting to quite like, held such offensive views, although I knew very well that he wouldn't be working at the Institute if he didn't.

The precepts that the Hiddwing Institute had been

created to declaim were couched in stirring patriotic language, but in essence included limited immigration — whites only, the forced repatriation of the present "inferior" immigrants and their children born in Australia to their originating countries, the limitation of voting rights to those who met the required racial, social, and financial qualifications, and genetic profiling to establish acceptable heritage before a citizen could be considered for government positions.

Jeffrey was casting sharp looks in my direction. Obviously something more was required of me. I said, my tone serious, "You know, I've always thought that it's better that people who have things in common should live in the same place. I mean, I've got nothing personally against, say, Vietnamese, but they should be in Vietnam. That's their home. And Australia's mine."

I saw him smile. "Exactly," he said.

I had the wry thought that if he knew my real opinions, he'd run the Volvo off into the bushes and take to me with a heavy object. Well, perhaps that was a bit extreme: He'd turf me out of the car, at least.

The traffic had thinned considerably once we'd turned onto a rather narrow two-lane highway, but Jeffrey continued to glance at the side and rear mirrors every few moments. The journey might not be exciting, but at least I could be confident of arriving at my destination in one piece.

"Hey," he said, "Elise is two cars behind us, if you want to check out her MGB." He made a disapproving noise. "Now she's one car behind. That woman has no idea how to drive safely."

I turned my head just as Elise Gordon roared past us on the wrong side of the road in her little green British sports car, the scarf holding her curly hair off her face whipping in the wind. Jeffrey braked as she abruptly darted in front of the Volvo to avoid an oncoming truck. Ignoring the blast of the truck driver's horn, she gave us a cheerful wave, then floored the MG and rapidly drew away from us.

"I'm glad I came with you," I said.

"Hmm." He sounded pleased.

I expected him to start a diatribe about Elise Gordon's driving. I was sure, in the same circumstances, that would be exactly what my brother would do, but Jeffrey changed the subject. "Did you find somewhere to live this afternoon?"

"Still looking. I saw a lot of flats, but . . ." I spread my hands.

"I share a house," he said. "It's in Paddington, not that far from work. Old wooden place, but it's been done up well. Four bedrooms, two bathrooms. All of us work at the Institute, and right now we've got a vacancy. Interested?"

"I don't think so."

"Of course, we'd have to do something with Vonny's things."

"Vonny?"

"Yeah. Vonny Quigley. Up until last month she worked at the Institute, then one day she just upped and left. Didn't bother to take most of her stuff, so it's still in her room. She has no family, so we don't know where to send it."

Outside the bush was growing thicker, the signs of civilization sparser. I imagined a lonely grave deep in the vegetation, and shivered. "Did you tell the cops she'd disappeared?"

He frowned at me. "Vonny didn't disappear. She called and said she was going, and she'd get back to us about her clothes and all. She never bothered, that's all." He turned smoothly off the road and onto a narrower way signposted PRIVATE ROAD NO ENTRY. "We're nearly there."

About half a kilometer in from the main road Jeffrey slowed to a stop at heavy iron gates. A bulky guard crammed in a tiny booth stepped out to look us over. "Jeffrey, you old bastard," he said, grinning, "what're you bench-pressing these days?"

I half listened to them trade gym jokes while I thought about Jeffrey's offer of a room. One of the advantages would be that I'd have a wonderful source of information, since everybody worked at the Institute. There were severe disadvantages, however, including the demands of playing my role twenty-four hours a day, and the difficulties of communication between Myra and myself, especially in an emergency. The Institute had sophisticated surveillance equipment — we'd seen it deployed in the past — and the chances of ongoing surveillance were much greater in established staff accommodations.

Jeffrey and the guard speedily broke off their conversation when a big Jaguar sedan pulled up behind the Volvo. "Heck," said Jeffrey, driving through the gateway, "we'd better hurry. That's Becky Hiddwing in the Jag."

The narrow roadway broadened into a drive illuminated by a series of metal lampposts that were facsimiles of antique gaslights. I was admiring the landscaping when Jeffrey said, "Well? What about the house? Your room would be one of the best ones, at the back away from any traffic noise."

"I don't know ... I'm a bit of a loner."

"You are?" He sounded astonished. "That's not what I'd peg you as."

"Deep down, I'm really quite shy."

"Oh, yeah? Must be a bit of a handicap if you're in public relations."

I had to concede that point, and it served me right for secretly having fun with him. "About the room," I said, "can I think about it, and tell you later?"

"Sure, no worries."

Jeffrey pulled smoothly up at the grand edifice of a substantial mansion, and a man in a white shirt and dark pants leapt forward to open my door.

I took a deep breath. Becky Hiddwing was getting out of the car behind us. Convincing her of my right-wing ardor was essential, but she was a formidable woman with a keen mind and rigorous judgment. I'd seen her countless times in the media, her palpable charm a veneer over her single-minded obsession to reform Australian society to fit her family's concept of racial purity.

Here was my first real test, and if I passed it, I'd be in with the in-crowd. If I failed, then my time with the Institute would be distressingly short.

CHAPTER FIVE

I had only a fleeting impression of Becky Hiddwing, as she wasted no time outside. She stepped out of her silver Jaguar, smiled charmingly at the man who had abandoned our ancient Volvo and had rushed to usher her out of her sleek vehicle, and then strode up the short flight of stone stairs and into the house.

"Wow. Some place," I said to Jeffrey.

He surveyed the two-story stone building as though he were its proud owner. "It is that. Eight bedrooms, each with a bathroom, banquet room, two large meeting rooms, library, computer room, gymnasium, game rooms, and huge kitchen, set up to serve hundreds, if necessary, and a huge patio out the back for entertaining. And there are separate cottages on the grounds to accommodate small parties of three or four."

"It certainly is impressive."

Jeffrey made an expansive gesture, taking in the whole facade of the building. "State-of-the-art communications, cutting-edge technology — nothing's been spared."

I'd seen the plans and knew the budget, so I was aware that Jeffrey was right — money had been no object. The ugly edifice in front of me had been designed by an architect with a taste for grandiose design and the benefit of an almost unlimited budget. The initial concept seemed to be taken from a Georgian country house in England and crossed with an ornate Victorian mansion. The result sat uncomfortably in the surrounding Australian bushland.

Constructed of granite, it loomed in stodgy grandeur, every one of its tall windows illuminated. Several spindly chimneys added a ridiculous touch, as though it were a gigantic gray cake decorated with grotesque candles.

"Come on," said Jeffrey, "it's even better inside."

"It is? That's hard to visualize."

Others had been arriving while we'd been talking, so we joined a knot of people and entered through the carved wooden door that sported, I was amused to see, a large brass door knocker in the shape of the Hiddwing burning torch, although this time it was held by a hand cut off at the wrist, contorted at an awkward angle so that the brass knuckles could hit the striker plate.

Jeffrey, mistaking my grin for appreciation of the entrance hall, said, "It *is* magnificent, isn't it."

Magnificent wasn't the word that leapt to mind: *pretentious* perhaps, or maybe *ostentatious*. A huge curved stone staircase dominated the area, and portraits of the founding brother and sister were featured at the first landing. Modern tapestries, each depicting some important historical event in the gospel according to Hiddwing hung on the walls — Captain Philip grandly claiming Australia for the British Empire caught my eye — and above us all a truly awesome chandelier hung like a gigantic, glittering stalactite. I hoped that its moorings were adequate. In my imagination I could see it doing a *Phantom of the Opera* descent into the throng below.

My fancies were broken by Elise Gordon, who jolted to a stop beside me as though she'd been running. She was wearing some sort of floral sari affair, her hair was tousled, no doubt from her sports car, and she had a flushed, jittery look that instantly made me want to tell her to calm down.

"Denise, glad you made it." She shot a look at Jeffrey. "Took you long enough to get here, but I'd say that was Jeffrey's fault."

"Better safe than sorry."

Elise made a face at him. "Better interesting than boring."

Jeffrey's face darkened. This had all the hallmarks of a frequent disagreement between them. "I'm hungry," I said brightly.

"Hungry? You can't eat yet. You have to meet Becky. She's been asking after you."

"After *me*?" I said with modest surprise.

Elise took my arm. "Becky knows everything that's going on, so don't ever try to fool her."

"I wouldn't dream of it."

Elise set off, towing me behind her. She was the type who steps on someone's toes, then expects the person to apologize to her. I kept saying, "Excuse me . . . sorry," while Elise plowed across the crowded entrance hall.

We went through double doors and into a spacious, wood-paneled room dominated by a large stone fireplace with a stone mantel and an arresting portrait of Becky Hiddwing above it. The woman herself, wearing a simple black dress, stood beneath the painting, holding court with at least twenty attentive people.

The only average things about Rhys Hiddwing's younger sister were her height and build. After that, she moved into the out-of-the-ordinary. In her the Hiddwing nose was still arrogant though shapely, the red hair a rich auburn, the heavy jaw a smooth and elegant curve. She gestured with casual grace, smiled often and warmly, and gave each speaker in turn her undivided, wide-eyed attention.

I knew she was ruthless, single-minded, and probably without conscience, but I expected to respect her as a worthy adversary, and perhaps I'd weaken and like her a little. Everybody did. Even dedicated foes melted when she turned the full force of her personality upon them. She was famous for de-fanging harsh interviewers and for fielding hard questions with persuasive replies.

Becky Hiddwing was also famous for her affairs. These were never blatant, but her high profile meant that they were never kept private for long either. She was known to swing both ways: Not that she'd ever admitted to bisexuality, but enough discarded lovers had been indiscreet to ensure public knowledge of her healthy appetites. She was unfailingly gracious about past partners, and had never publicly criticized any of them, even those who had broken faith and talked to the media.

Her proclivities were possibly the reason that the Hiddwing Institute, unlike most extreme right-wing organizations, did not trumpet the so-called "family values" position, nor did it condemn homosexuality. For all that enlightened stance, the rest of the Institute's teachings were virulently racist. It was made very clear that sexual relationships between the races were totally unacceptable if one of the parties happened to be Caucasian. Apparently anything went if you were black, yellow, or brown — the restrictions only applied to whites.

Ilka stood beside Becky, playing, I thought, a sort of Teutonic handmaiden. She took Becky's empty champagne flute and deftly replaced it with another full of sparkling wine.

"Ilka!" Beside me Elise was waving energetically.

Ilka caught sight of us, frowned, then bent to say something to Becky. The effect of this was flattering: Becky Hiddwing looked up, smiled brilliantly in our direction, handed her glass to Ilka, patted the shoulder of the person she'd been talking with, and came over to us.

"Elise, I've been meaning to tell you how much I like your work on the mercy-killing issue." She turned her attention to me. "Denise Brandt. What a pleasure it is to have you join us at the Institute. I've heard great things from Frank Radon and Tansey Yates."

My cue for a demure smile. "Thank you."

"Of course," said Becky Hiddwing, grinning, "there's an element of self-interest in everything our Tansey says."

I blinked. She laughed at my reaction. "I've surprised you? Surely you're aware that Tansey likes her staff to burn a little less brightly than she does herself?"

"Well . . ."

"Don't waste time being modest, Denise. I know very well how good you are. I expect excellence, and I reward it."

"I like that." I made the statement simple and sincere.

Smiling, she nodded approval. "Good, then we understand each other. We'll be working together on several projects, and I must say how much I'm looking forward to the experience."

Meeting her in person helped me understand why so many people were putty in her hands — hands, incidentally, that were long, slender, and beautifully manicured.

"I liked your work on the Frick problem," she said. "A difficult situation that you handled well."

I murmured something appropriate, thinking of Byford Frick's fleshy, self-satisfied face. I had loathed the man from the moment I had taken over PR regarding his "little problem," as he called it. An outspoken fundamentalist clergyman who was a shameless media hog, but also one of the Institute's greatest supporters, he had had the misfortune to be arrested soliciting an underage female prostitute. There was the usual media frenzy, with the Reverend Frick's name, face, and close association with the Hiddwings splashed all over.

I'd engineered a media blitz right back, concentrating on heartwarming stories about his work with troubled youth — some of it, fortunately, true — and had floated the story that he was on the streets at two in the morning looking for young souls to save.

To my secret amazement the charges were eventually dropped, and a new, juicy scandal involving a pop group, its rabid teenage fan club, and certain mothers of said teenage fans, swept Frick's ordeal out of the public mind.

"I imagine you found Byford Frick quite distasteful," said Becky, her face serious. "I, myself, can't stand the man, but for the good of the Institute we have to deal with people we would never have as even a distant acquaintance. I'd like to thank you for your skill and grace."

She was buttering me up in a shameless fashion, and I found myself liking it. Her psychological profile indicated that she was a control freak who needed to know the minutiae of the organization and its activities. It hadn't indicated that she could charm the birds out of the trees.

Ilka materialized, still holding the champagne glass. "Becky, Gustave Zeeman has just arrived."

Her tone indicated this was an event of some importance, wholly justified, since Zeeman was a rising political star in the federal government, and was seen by many as future prime minister material.

"Please excuse me," she said to both of us, then turned back to say to me, "Perhaps we can have a meeting tomorrow in my office. Would seven be okay?" Her lips curved. "That would be seven in the morning."

It wasn't strictly true, but I'd noted the friendly scorn early risers had toward night owls who slept in, so I said, "I always get up early, so seven is fine by me."

Becky moved away, pausing for a moment here and there to greet someone or other. Beside me, Elise said, "You've made a good impression. Wise move."

"I'm in PR. I *always* try to make a good impression."

Elise's smile was sardonic. "Is that so?" Someone caught her attention. "God, there's Penelope Naughton. She's a big supporter, but she needs regular soothing. Can you look after yourself?"

"Sure."

I watched Elise make a beeline for a large woman with a discontented face and a frilly pink outfit. Reaching her, Elise exclaimed, "Penelope! Thank God you're here. At last someone interesting to talk to."

Penelope didn't look the slightest bit interesting to me, but she was delighted to be told this, and her petulant mouth formed a reluctant smile.

"Been abandoned?" said a voice beside me. It was Rhys Hiddwing. He put a hand on my elbow. Somehow his red hair seemed redder, his hooked nose more hooked. I willed him not to mention anything about having seen me somewhere before, since I hadn't yet got the information necessary for my cover story, but all he said was, "Follow me. We've got a barbecue set up on the rear patio, and, apart from food, there are several people you should meet."

Obedient, I trotted behind him as he made his way

through a dizzying succession of rooms and hallways filled with people and the buzz of conversation. The same questionable taste that had been in evidence in the entry hall had obviously been responsible for furnishing the whole house.

Seeing me looking around, Rhys said, "Awful, isn't it?"

Disconcerted for the second time in a few minutes by a Hiddwing, I said lamely, "It is a bit overwhelming . . ."

He gave a snort of laughter. "It's bloody hideous," he said. "I made the mistake of giving Ilka and my sister a free hand."

I thought of the elegant Becky Hiddwing. "Your sister?"

"I have to admit she was working with my father and aunt's vision for the place, and neither one of them had any taste at all when it came to architecture or interior decorating."

I gazed at a sideboard in the room we were traversing. It was elaborately carved, but breathtakingly ugly. "So you'd do it a little differently?" I said.

"Too right! My own apartment on the top floor bears no resemblance to this, I can tell you."

He broke off as we came through French windows and out onto an expansive patio. The smell of cooking steaks filled the warm, summer air, and my stomach reminded me that I'd skipped lunch.

Rhys took my arm to guide me toward a knot of people by the bar. "You must meet Sid Warde, our head of security."

Just as Becky Hiddwing's photographs didn't show the weight of her personality, Sid Warde's failed to indicate the controlled menace that surrounded him like an aura. Dressed entirely in black, he was only a little taller than me, and his tough, muscled body matched his hard face. Balding, he'd shaved off the remaining fringe of hair, and the bare skin of his skull shone like a polished stone.

"Sid," said Rhys Hiddwing, "this is Denise Brandt. Denise — Sid Warde."

Predictably, the pressure of his handshake was just this side of painful. His mouth smiled, his narrow blue eyes remained cold.

"Denise," he said in a gravel voice, "I have an interesting security file on you."

My heart flipped. Had ASIO slipped up somewhere? "Oh?" I said, eyebrows raised.

"Yes." He put his face a little closer to mine. "Interesting for what it *doesn't* say, rather than for what it does."

CHAPTER SIX

A burst of laughter came from the group gathered around one of the liquor bars; the light breeze was warm, but I felt a prickle of cold. Maintaining an expression that I hoped showed polite inquiry and not the alarm I felt, I murmured, "Really?"

Rhys said, "What's that supposed to mean?"

Sid Warde shrugged. "You don't appear to have done all that much, Denise."

Muted indignation seemed the way to go. "Not done much? I believe I've got what I'd call, in all modesty, an excellent work history."

"Work history?" Sid gave a small nod of acknowledgment. "You've certainly got that. It's commitment to the cause I find curiously lacking — membership in groups sympathetic to our aims, a role in protest movements, some association with organizations who share the right values."

I mentally cursed myself. In the early stages of planning for this undercover job, Myra had mentioned this very issue, and I'd airily said to her, "We don't need to do much in that line, because they'll never bother to go *that* deep. They'll just be interested in my PR skills." Now my words were coming back to haunt me.

Both Rhys and Sid were watching me with interrogative expressions, so some convincing response was required.

"I *have* done some stuff, especially at university, but I admit not much. I suppose it's because I'm a bit of a lone wolf."

Sid cocked his head. "How so?"

"I've never been a joiner, you know what I mean? And there's a bit too much of a social element in those groups, at least for someone like me, so I've always preferred to support our cause in other ways."

I worried that saying "our cause" might be pushing it, but Rhys was smiling at me. "I have to agree with Denise," he said. "Activists are essential, of course, but sheer hard work behind the scenes is vital too. Without that unsung effort, all the public demonstrations in the world will achieve very little in practical terms."

Sid's lips stretched in a closed-mouth semismile. "Uh-huh," he said, appearing not the least convinced.

"Perhaps, Denise, we can discuss it further at some later date."

"Be glad to." I didn't sound eager, but with Rhys siding with me, my reckoning was that I didn't have to be enthusiastic.

A young man, fully as hard in body and face as Sid, came to mutter something in Sid's ear. He nodded, then said to us, "Security breach. No big deal — just someone who's wandered onto the estate, but I'd like to deal with it personally."

I was already feeling sorry for whoever it was.

Watching Sid Warde walk away with a panther stride, I had to remind myself not to be intimidated by him. So Sid was assessed as dangerous, so he had black belts in a variety of martial arts — I was pretty dangerous myself. Well . . . at least somewhat hazardous.

Rhys had taken my arm again, in a gentle, guiding grasp. I wondered for the first time if this touching thing was at all lecherous. Too bad if it was: I was in no position to scream "Sexual harassment!"

With pride he surveyed the patio, where up to a hundred people were gathered in small groups. Some were seated at tables, eating — my stomach rumbled — others were clustered around the row of barbecue grills or filling their plates at tables loaded with salads and bread, or milling around one of the three bars.

I had a nostalgic flash of my time undercover as a bartender, but resolutely shoved the thought away. Such memories opened too many distracting images from the past, not to mention unspecific hopes for the future.

"It's wonderful, isn't it?" said Rhys. "All these

people who believe strongly in what we stand for, all assembled together." He looked down at me, his eyes filled with zeal. "It's the energy that such a gathering creates that is the driving force of the Hiddwing Institute."

As I reflected that Ilka was obviously not the only one prone to speechify at any given moment, the woman herself approached us, her face set in serious lines. "Rhys, Becky asks will you join her and Gustave in the library immediately, please?"

"A problem?"

She looked at me. "Could be."

Hell, was that an oblique reference to me? My nerves certainly weren't going to be in good shape if I kept getting jolts like this. Of course, there was every possibility that I was paranoid and that Ilka was merely hesitating to mention something confidential in front of a new employee.

Rhys Hiddwing excused himself and hurried toward the house. For a big man, he moved easily through the crowded space. I glanced at Ilka. She was watching him too, and her expression showed unguarded longing.

Hello. Something intelligence didn't pick up here.

"Quite a guy," I said, my voice warm.

My comment was not welcome. Ilka's eyes narrowed. "Yes, he is," she said coldly.

Deciding it probably wasn't a good idea to have her treating me as a rival for the object of her affections, I said, "But not my type."

She gave me a long stare. "And what *is* your type, Denise?"

"Oh, I don't know . . . someone different. You might

say idiosyncratic, but basically a lot of fun to be with."

This conversation wasn't going well. She frowned at me. "You won't find anyone like that at the Institute. Here we all think the same, believe the same, follow the true path."

Sigh. Ilka was hopping on her soapbox again.

I was saved — if falling from the frying pan into the fire is that — by the surly-faced Penelope Naughton, whom Elise earlier had gone to soothe. "I don't know you, do I?" the woman said in an accusatory tone, as if I had deliberately set out to keep her in the dark.

I hesitated, always wary of a slip. As I was using my own first name, I had to guard against the tendency to add my real last name. Myra, of course, had pointed this out, so I'd vowed to be super careful.

So get the name right.

"I'm Denise Brandt, and new at the Institute. I came from the Melbourne branch."

My reply didn't lift her sour expression. "Is that so?"

I looked to Ilka for help, but clearly she had met Penelope before, as she mumbled something about having to do something, and escaped, leaving me trapped.

"I'm in public relations," I said. I made an obvious show of looking around, as though an opportunity for PR might present itself any moment. "It's so exciting to see so many important people here, all in one place."

"You've heard of me? Penelope Naughton?"

I hadn't. "The name's familiar . . ."

63

Her heavy face solidified in a combination of ire and disbelief. "Naughton pens," she said loudly, working on the principle that I would understand more clearly if she bellowed. "My late husband founded the company and built it, with my help, to the industry leader it is today."

A couple passing by looked at her in surprise, then at me. I didn't blame them when they accelerated their pace.

"Of course," I said, resisting the impulse to slap myself on the forehead like a dim yokel. "Naughton pens."

"You probably use them every day."

Naughton pens, as I now recalled, were mass-produced ballpoints with iridescent barrels. I'd found they had a penchant to run out after only a short time of use. "Use them every day," I repeated dutifully.

Penelope was inclined to be nice, now that she'd set me straight. "I know everyone who's anyone," she said. "Just point the person out, and I'll give you the lowdown."

Because it was very likely that the Hiddwings had covert supporters that ASIO had not yet detected, from the time I'd arrived at the Hiddwing Estate I'd been mentally listing every celebrity or business notable that I'd recognized. Penelope, if she spoke the truth, could be a valuable source of further information.

"Okay," I said, "who's that guy over there at the table with Ursula Philips and her husband?" Ursula Philips was one of Australia's premier actors, and her most recent LA movie, *Shrieks in the Night*, had given her an international recognition factor.

Penelope squinted in that direction. "The man with the unfortunate haircut? Lawrence Erman, the high court judge."

Running a quick check of known associates of the Hiddwings, no judge of Australia's high court popped up, so this was a find. "Hey," I said with genuine admiration, "you're good at this."

Penelope wiggled her pink-clad shoulders, clearly pleased. "Anyone else?" she said, relishing the challenge.

"Have you eaten?" I asked hopefully. If I didn't get food soon, my knees would buckle.

"I don't like barbecues," Penelope announced. She startled me with a sudden bark of laughter. "As my late husband used to say, a barbecue is either a burnt offering or a bloody sacrifice."

"He must have been a wit."

Her face grew grim. "He was quite boring, actually," she said. "Pens, pens, pens. That's all he ever talked about. Morning, noon, and night. Pens."

"Not much variety there."

She gave me a suspicious glance, but I made sure my face didn't reveal the slightest humor.

"Have you met Axel Dorca?"

I looked at her with new respect. Dorca was a young dot-com entrepreneur whose company's value had gone from nothing to a billion dollars in what seemed no time flat. "Friend of my son's," said Penelope. "Don't understand a thing about his business, but he's a polite young man." Her mouth turned down. "At least, to my face he is. Who knows what he says behind my back."

She pointed. "There's Axel over there. He's talking with Helena."

My antennae went up. Helena Court-Howerd was so influential in political circles that she was known, not entirely affectionately, as the Queensland Kingmaker. Kingmaker was a misnomer, as she was an equal opportunity patron, and had promoted the careers of both men and women, the only requirement being that the person come from the entirely fanatical far-right-of-Hitler school of thinking. When I thought about it, it was depressing how many candidates vying for her support there were.

"You know Helena Court-Howerd?" I said in tones of admiration.

"Of course. I'll introduce you, if you like."

Penelope sailed in that direction, and I followed like a small tugboat after a liner. She dropped anchor, breaking into their conversation without apology. "Helena, Axel — you're to meet . . ."

Penelope trailed off and glared at me, having forgotten my name.

"Denise Brandt," I said. "I'm new at the Institute. I've been working at the Melbourne branch."

Axel Dorca was jockey-sized, an alert terrier of a man. I expected his tongue to loll out of his mouth at any moment. "Well, hello!" he exclaimed, looking me up and down with almost comical lasciviousness.

He took my arm — that appendage seemed to be a magnet for attention this evening — and smiled up into my face. "Just arrived in Brisbane?" he inquired. "Probably feeling a bit lonely, are you?"

"Not lonely at all."

"Pity." He showed a little more of his fine, white teeth. "A pretty girl like you."

"Pay no attention," said Penelope scathingly. "Axel

does this with every female, though God knows, he could buy whomever he wanted."

"I'm not for sale," I said.

Helena Court-Howerd gave a genteel snort. "I should hope not."

She was stick-thin, high-cheekboned, and the recipient, it was rumored, of extensive face work. Her best features were her large, slightly bulbous blue eyes and her upright carriage. She was smoking with a long black cigarette holder — one of her affectations. The other was her manner of speaking, always very much in evidence in television interviews. She had a drawling delivery with a sudden speed-up at the end of sentences, which gave the effect of a verbal rubber band stretched to the limit, then snapping back.

She surveyed me with vague interest, and said, "And what, actually, do you *do?*"

"Anything necessary."

Axel giggled and rolled his eyes. A quick slap would have satisfied me, but instead I gave him a bemused look.

Helena obviously liked my snappy reply. A smile flickered across her gaunt face. "Excellent," she said. "I gather you're a woman of no scruples."

"A few finely-honed ones."

Penelope, growing bored with the conversation, cleared her throat. "Helena, we must discuss the Hawkins fund-raiser."

Helena, looking around with a frown, paid no attention. I could feel it too — there'd been some subtle shift in the mood of the party. Some people were on cell phones, others were talking in urgent tones.

"Something's up," she said.

As she spoke, Rhys Hiddwing came out of the house. "May I have your attention?" he said. I realized his voice was amplified, as it carried to every corner of the patio.

The buzz of conversation stilled. He waited for a moment, then said, "There's been an attempt on the prime minister's life. No details, but he's apparently been shot, and his condition is grave."

CHAPTER SEVEN

I ordered room-service breakfast for an indecently early hour, even though I'd gobbled down a T-bone steak quite late in the evening, and didn't really feel hungry. I had that seven o'clock appointment with Becky Hiddwing, and needed strong coffee to clear my head before I faced her. I was determined, if possible, to be at least a few minutes early.

Flicking around television channels as I consumed black coffee and an excellent cheese omelet, I found each broadcast was pretty much the same — harried presenters trying to find something new to say, or a new way to give the same old information. Last night Jeffrey and I had barely spoken as we'd listened to the car radio on the way home, and this morning the media had little to add to what we'd heard then, although the shock that something like this had happened in Australia had sunk in, and comments like "unthinkable that it should happen here" and "previously immune to political violence" were now being bandied about.

Albert Paggi, Australia's prime minister for the last four years, had been shot several times as he left a reception for a visiting Indonesian minister at an upscale Sydney hotel. The spray of bullets had also wounded the Indonesian minister's bodyguard and killed a federal cop who had been flanking the official party as they came out to the waiting limousines.

This morning there'd been some halfhearted speculation that the assassination attempt could have been aimed at the foreign visitor, but there wasn't much to pursue with this angle, as the evidence pointed to the fact that Paggi had been the intended target. Witnesses had confirmed that the two-person assassination team had shouted "Traitor to your race!" as they had surged out of the crowd, firing handguns. The man and woman, unidentified as yet, had been detained nearby, but had, it was reported, refused to make any statements. Predictably, an inquiry into security arrangements for public figures had been announced by the Deputy Prime Minister, Heath Abbottson.

The attack had meant that Albert Paggi was receiving more concentrated attention than he had ever gained during his four rather uninspiring years in power. High points of his career — not all that many — were examined, and his life was exhaustively mined, with emphasis on his background and the fact that, although he'd been born in Australia, his family had originally come from Italy shortly after World War Two. His elderly parents, both still living, were immediately descended upon by the ravening hordes of the media. Paggi's wife and two sons had better protection: News editors had to be content with long shots as they hurried into the hospital to which Paggi had been rushed.

Hourly bulletins were being issued, but there was little variation in them. The PM had survived extensive surgery to remove bullet fragments, part of his liver, and all of his spleen. He was in critical, but stable, condition.

I'd never thought much one way or the other about Paggi. He was a gray sort of man, without any burning convictions save one: He was markedly pro-immigration. Possibly this was because his parents had been immigrants, part of the flood of displaced people looking for new homes and new hopes after the devastation of war. Whatever the reason, he had raised the ire of organizations like Australia for Whites Alone, a radical bunch who had found the Internet a wonderful boon, and who were one of the most malignant of the poisonous hate groups that used race as an issue.

In the past the Hiddwing Institute had been more politic, but just as harsh, in its evaluation of Paggi. The statement that Paggi was "a betrayer of his genetic heritage" was the strongest comment made, but the essential message was the same.

I checked the time, swore, and bolted into the bathroom to clean my teeth. Fifteen minutes later I was in my rental car and zipping through light traffic in the direction of the Institute. As I drove, I thought of last night and the overall reaction to the news Rhys Hiddwing had unceremoniously announced.

There'd been a babble of conversation when it became clear he had nothing else to add to the bald statement. Near me, someone had actually laughed, and I'd also heard a couple of "serves the bastard right" comments.

Helena Court-Howerd had been impassive, merely pressing a new cigarette into her long holder. Penelope Naughton had tut-tutted, more with what's-the-world-coming-to than with regret. Axel Dorca had snatched out his mobile phone with the terse comment, "Jesus, this'll impact on the markets big time!"

Some called out: "Who did it?"

Rhys had lifted his shoulders. "Who knows? The man had enemies."

I remembered the hollow feeling I'd had in my stomach, and it wasn't just lack of food. With cold certainty, I knew that somehow the Hiddwings, if not directly involved in the assassination attempt, wholly supported it. I imagined there was some disappointment that it had not been a complete success.

As I drove, I looked around the clean Brisbane city streets, felt the balmy air of another lazy summer day kiss my face through the car's open window, and wanted to believe that the dark theories of over-throwing the government from within were wildly exaggerated. I'd liked both Rhys and Becky when I'd met them, was amused by Elise and Jeffrey, and could even smile at Ilka, as long as I had her in small doses. Then I thought of Sid Warde, and the bleak possibilities didn't seem so farfetched after all.

In contrast to the architectural horror that was the Hiddwing estate, the Institute office building was all sleek modernism. I gazed at its tinted glass walls and wondered about the secrets — and the dangers — inside. The entrance to the underground parking was off a laneway at the rear, and, as a new and lowly employee, I'd been assigned a parking spot at the very bottom of the structure. The security guard examined my temporary identification card closely — later today I would be given a permanent plastic card with a laminated photograph. I'd already memorized my numerical password that allowed me to enter most areas of the building.

Once through the boomgate, I spiraled down into the lowest levels, thinking of the sunshine disappearing behind me. My involuntary shiver was the product of an overactive imagination as I visualized myself sinking lower and lower into a concrete underworld.

Finding the narrow slot that was to be mine, I parked, grabbed my near-empty briefcase, and got out of the car into a deserted, echoing space that seemed to hum with menace. The air was hot and still, and smelled of oily concrete and car exhausts. Naturally my assigned parking spot was a long way from the exit. I looked around. This was a perfect place for an attack — no one would hear or see anything. I could almost see my lifeless body slumped against the nearest supporting column. A quick check of my watch let me give myself permission to really hurry, although I knew I would have moved just as rapidly even if I'd had plenty of time.

In my mind's eye I could see Myra smiling at me. She had always said that the ability to visualize scenarios was an invaluable tool in an agent, but that in my case I tended to take it to extremes.

Last night I'd wanted to call her as soon as Jeffrey dropped me off at my hotel, not only to give my report on the evening at the estate, but, more importantly, to get the details of my cover story for Rhys Hiddwing. Unfortunately it was the worst possible time to call Myra. After news like the attempt on the prime minister's life, an agent would be expected to contact base, and therefore, if I were being watched, any use of a public phone late at night would be recorded as unusual behavior. And I didn't want anyone thinking I was at all unusual — at least not in that sense. To be a little different personally could be an advantage: How could anyone think a plant was calling attention to herself that way?

Well, that's how I'd explained it to my trainer, who'd been drilling me in office procedures for public relations executives, and had complained about my rather original approach. He'd rolled his eyes — he often did that with me — and said, "A little unusual is okay, Denise. Downright odd is not."

I heard a car door slam some distance away, and quickened my steps. I have a mini-phobia about lifts — I always have a sneaking idea at the back of my brain that they will get stuck between floors and leave me trapped, probably in the company of a psychopath — so I chose the iron fire stairs instead, and clattered up to the ground floor level as though someone, or something, pursued me.

The lobby was entirely empty and filled with deliciously cold air. I hastened across the expanse of gray tiles toward the executive wing, wondering how I was going to get in through the security door, as I hadn't been deemed worthy of a personal code to punch into the keypad.

"You're barely on time," said Ilka, the living answer to my silent query. She was severe in a navy tailored suit, making me feel rather too colorful in my aqua outfit. She patted her pale chignon, although it was clear to me not a hair would dare to be out of place. "We'll go right through."

Concentrating on her fingers, I got the last three digits of the security code. Added to the first three I'd caught yesterday, this meant that, unless the code changed regularly, I now had means of entry into the executive offices. I glanced up: An almost imperceptible lens was set into the wall above the door. If I did get in, my entry would be recorded.

Ilka led the way down the thick beige carpet at her usual fast clip. "Becky has been here at the Institute since six," she said with pride. "I, myself, since five."

When I looked suitably impressed she acknowledged this with a quick duck of her head. "You, too, will be expected to keep early hours."

"And work late?" A polite inquiry, not a complaint.

"Of course."

"I'm looking for a place to stay. I had hoped to get off a little early . . ."

She drew her thin eyebrows together. "Jeffrey's offered you a room."

It was surprising that my living arrangements were of such general interest. I said, "Yesterday Will Hiddwing sort of hinted that living in the same house with Jeffrey would be a trial."

"Nonsense. Will doesn't know what he's talking about, as usual. Jeffrey may have his faults, but he's basically steady and reliable. And the others sharing the house with him are employed here at the Institute. I think it an excellent idea."

Well, I'll rush out and do it straightaway. Aloud, I said, "Maybe . . ."

"Decisiveness is a paramount quality."

I could feel a lecture coming on, but fortunately we'd reached Becky Hiddwing's open office door. She looked up from her desk and beckoned us in. She was in crisp white and seemed quite rested, although I was sure she'd had less sleep than I'd had. "Good of you to come in so early, Denise. There's coffee over by the window. Help yourself."

Although I was aslosh with coffee from breakfast, having gulped down an entire large pot, I put down my briefcase and went over and got a mug. I felt unaccountably nervous and wanted something to occupy my hands.

Rhys Hiddwing's office was furnished in light-hued cane and filled with light; his sister's featured dark furniture and heavy drapes, through which only dim light filtered. Illumination came from an undoubtedly expensive Tiffany lamp on the desk and a matching floor lamp in one corner of the room.

Clutching my mug, I seated myself in front of Becky's desk, took a notepad from my briefcase, and assumed a look of attentive, bright-eyed eagerness. Ilka chose a companion chair, sitting on the edge so that she was poised to leap to her feet to fulfil Becky's instructions.

Becky rested her elegant chin on linked fingers and regarded me somberly. With an expression of distaste, she said, "Have you heard of Australia's Redemption?"

I had, but only in the preparation for this assignment. Australia's Redemption was a very small, very fanatical group of mainly young people who had at their core a belief, possibly justified, that the British had illegally seized the country from the tribal Aborigines, who'd had a prior history of forty thousand years of occupation of the continent. In a leap of logic I didn't quite understand, AR proposed that in absolution for this infamous act two hundred years ago, all barriers to immigration be immediately lifted, so that anyone who wished to enter Australia could do so without restraint. It went without saying that the Hiddwing Institute was the group's arch enemy, but the AR was rather like a flea declaring war on an elephant.

"They're some bunch of fanatics, aren't they?" I said.

"During the night we received a telephoned death threat from Australia's Redemption against Rhys and myself, and all our employees." She seemed irritated, rather than alarmed.

"You've reported it to the police?"

Becky threw up her hands in a gesture of disgust. "The Queensland cops? What would they do that was useful?" She shook her head. "Sid's looking after the problem. He's asked that everyone in the Institute be particularly careful, just in case one of these cranks gets up the courage to do something."

"I'll be careful."

"You're staying in a hotel, aren't you?"

I had a premonition that Jeffrey was about to be mentioned. "Yes, just until I find a flat."

"I'd like you to move into the house that Jeffrey Karl is renting. I believe he's mentioned he has a vacancy to you."

This interest from Becky Hiddwing in my accommodations was surprising, and rather alarming. Maybe the Hiddwings did have suspicions and wanted me where they could keep a close eye on my activities. Hell, they could have every room bugged with video and audio, for all I knew.

"I'd rather have a place of my own."

"Humor me," said Becky with the most charming of smiles. "I'm worried about my staff, and you're a stranger here and very exposed in a hotel. How about you move in just for a few days, while Sid's assessing the threat to the Institute? Then, I promise you, if you still want to move, I'll arrange for you to get somewhere suitable."

"I'll certainly think about it."

"Excellent." Becky acted as though I'd agreed with her instructions. "Now, to other business. This Paggi situation is a public relations matter of some urgency. I'm sure you share our pleasure and relief that some-one with such dangerous views has been removed from power, at least temporarily, but we can hardly come out and say that officially. I think our media release should emphasize our beliefs while expressing the usual shock and horror at the use of violence in our society."

"It's an excellent opportunity," I said, "to capitalize on the situation."

Becky raised her eyebrows. "You think so?"

"I do." I almost convinced myself with the

certitude in my voice. I'd given this some thought, but I was basically winging it here. "You've already had a lot of requests for comments on the shooting? Yes?"

Becky sighed. "The bullets had hardly been fired before we had reporters asking for our comments. We now have a recording saying that the Institute will make an official statement later today at a media conference."

"It's not enough," I said. "Left-wing media people will try to paint the Hiddwing Institute in the worst possible light. They'll hint that it's our fault that an assassination attempt was made on Albert Paggi — that we created an atmosphere of hate and dissension that encouraged the attack."

In my mind it was entirely true that the Institute had done that, and more, but I did manage a convincing note of righteous indignation as I continued, "I believe we have to take the offensive here. I'm suggesting that you seize the initiative and beat the left-wingers to the punch."

Ilka's fingers drummed a tattoo on the folder she held. "I don't agree —"

Becky silenced her with a gesture. "Go on, Denise."

"Take the battle up to their gates," I said. "I've watched the coverage. The channels are desperate for something fresh to add to the mix, and this is where you and Rhys come in. Have the media conference if you must, but first make yourself available from this moment on for any interview, any appearance on a news show."

"I must object to this, Becky." Ilka's tone was strident. "What Denise is suggesting is that you and Rhys set yourself up as targets for any little reporter to criticize. It's not wise to give them such opportunities. I'm against the whole idea."

I gave a rueful shrug. "Becky, you can handle any interviewer with ease, no matter what the situation. It seems a pity to let such a chance to reach a mass audience go by without taking advantage of it."

Becky was ready to be persuaded. "Let's hear some specifics."

Launching into my hard sell, I realized that I was having fun creating on the fly. I heard the warmth of enthusiasm in my voice and found that I was convincing myself as well as Becky. Her body language was positive as I explained the value of being proactive rather than reactive, of how the presentation of the polished, patriotic face of the Institute in the best possible light would frustrate the attacks of the pro-immigration, anti-Hiddwing factions.

Hey, I wouldn't be half bad at public relations, if ASIO ever pensions me off.

"I'll go for it," said Becky, showing the admirable decisiveness that Ilka had extolled a few minutes before. "Ilka, find Rhys, wherever he is, and tell him we have to meet immediately."

"But —"

"No buts. Just do it."

Ilka stomped out of the office. Becky grinned. "We've upset her. She likes to play it safe, always."

Not wanting to be seen criticizing Ilka, I said, "Safe is generally a good way to go."

"Oh no, Denise," said Becky, her smile widening. "I believe you'll find quite the opposite, where I'm concerned. *Quite* the opposite."

CHAPTER EIGHT

Installed in a small, glass-walled office, I spent the day in a blur of telephone calls and urgent messages. I had the media contact list I'd inherited from the guy I'd replaced, plus my own files of national network connections that I'd compiled while working in Melbourne. Of course, personnel changed at television and radio stations, which meant that getting to that one key person was often a game of hit and miss. Nevertheless, I'd managed to book both Becky and Rhys for a goodly number of appearances with well-respected news programs and had had the satisfaction of watching the noon news feature the Hiddwing brother and sister in a positive interview.

Ilka was in and out, efficient but displeased. I was leaning back, enjoying a welcome lull in the calls, when she marched in, put her hands on the edge of my desk, and leaned over me to say, "You should know that this is an aberration. Prior to this, Becky and Rhys have always listened to my advice."

I looked up at her admirable jaw, and visualized her snapping off my head with one bite of her excellent white teeth. "These are unusual circumstances —"

"All the more reason why my opinions should be given weight." Her expression became more militant, a precursor, I'd learned, that a lecture was about to begin.

"Continuity," she announced, "continuity and consistency. Advice taken from tried and true sources should have precedence over —" She broke off to glower at me. "Inexperience."

"Ilka, I'm sorry you're upset, but I do have a background in public relations, and I suggested what in my judgment was the most advantageous strategy."

Jeez, I was beginning to sound like her.

Her expression grudging, she said, "The overall effect does seem to be a positive one."

Mercifully the phone rang, so I could break off the conversation with a valid excuse. Ilka strode out of the office as though embarking on a long hike, to be replaced by Crystal, one of my two young assistants, who had a sheaf of papers for me to read. This was starting to feel like a real job, and a hard one, at that.

With a receiver clamped to my aching ear, I was

waiting on hold for the producer of *The Shipley Report* newsmagazine to come on the line when Elise bounced in to slap a typed page in front of me.

"Hey, Elise, I'm flat-out like a lizard drinking, here!" I didn't mean to speak sharply, but I was tired, I'd had no time for lunch, and I still had a stack of calls to return.

"It's not *my* idea," said Elise, pouting. Her bracelets jangled as she punched a forefinger into the center of the page. "Read and initial. Crazy as it sounds, you've got to okay this. Becky's orders."

"So what is it?"

"Oh, God!" Elise wriggled her shoulders so that the flounces on her flowery top trembled. "It's bloody annoying, I can tell you, but Becky's got it into her head that you're some kind of wonder woman."

The corners of Elise's mouth went down as I gave a don't-blame-me shrug. "Not your fault," she said, sounding as though it most certainly was, "but Becky says nothing goes onto the Web site unless you vet it first. This is a response to the Paggi thing. Standard stuff — shocked at violence, but the PM's unreasonable stand on immigration has led to instability, blah-blah-blah. Just say it's okay, and I'll get out of your hair."

Elise was responsible for the Hiddwing Web site, e-mail correspondence from the public, and Internet links to organizations sharing the Institute's political and social policies. I was very familiar with the Web site, which was excellently designed, with sharp, clean images and an imaginative, effective structure.

I skimmed the printout quickly. It was good: crisp and to the point. The phone came alive in my ear as

I scribbled my initials, remembering at the last moment that I was supposed to be putting *DB* and not *DC*.

As I started my pitch to the producer, who'd finally come to the phone, I handed the page back to Elise. I made a mental note to mend fences with her later. It would only make things more difficult if she started to regard me as an enemy.

By late afternoon I felt totally exhausted but pleased with myself for a job well done. Radio and television slots had been filled, and the Hiddwing Institute was in the process of getting a positive PR image from an event that had had the potential to be very damaging to the cause, especially if the prime minister died.

This was a distinct possibility, as Paggi was still listed as extremely critical. The two television sets in my office had been on all day, so between calls I'd picked up news bulletins on both the PM's condition and the investigation into his attempted assassination. Neither of his two assailants had been identified. Both had apparently claimed that Australia's law enforcement had no authority over them and then refused to say anything more.

I was sipping a mug of coffee that one of my staff — I had to smile to myself at that term — had just brought me when Sid Warde, carrying a clipboard, came into my office and sat down. His tight black trousers, fitted black short-sleeved shirt, and shaved head combined to give him a threatening air. His face expressionless, he stared at me with unblinking blue eyes.

My pulse jumped. I wasn't used to being this apprehensive about anybody, and reassured myself it was because I was hungry and bone tired. Even a quick reminder that his code name was the entirely inappropriate *Hummingbird* didn't help. "Hi, Sid. What can I do for you?"

"Tell me the truth."

"It'll be difficult. I'm a pathological liar."

That made the bastard blink.

"Really?"

"Just joking. What truth do you want in particular?"

He flicked the folder open. "This is a copy of your job application for the position in our Melbourne branch."

I comforted myself that there could be nothing in it that could hurt me, as painstaking efforts had been made to make everything ring true. "You've caught me out," I said, looking penitent. "I said I like team sports, and I don't really. Just put it in because it sounded like the sort of thing that would make a good impression."

"You do this often? Make up things?" The timbre of his voice grated unpleasantly, reminding me of pebbles rattling in tin.

"Often?" I said in mock surprise. "I do it all the time. It's my job, for heaven's sake. What is PR but putting the best spin on things?"

His thin lips twitched with a faint suggestion of amusement. "Smart answer. You're pretty sharp, Denise."

With a knowing smile, I said, "You just came in to frighten me, didn't you, with all this stuff about telling the truth and my job application?"

Sid sucked in his cheeks, then startled me by actually smiling. "And *did* I frighten you?"

"Scared shitless," I said cheerfully. "But then, I'm very easy to alarm."

He cocked his head, his narrow eyes intent. "Somehow I doubt that."

"It's true. Scare me enough and I'll shriek and run around. I could star in a horror movie, no prob."

Stop it, Denise. Don't embroider too much.

Sid leaned over the desk to hand me a small plastic rectangle. "This is what I'm here for — to give you your ID card."

Yesterday I'd thought the Polaroid shot of me was very unflattering. Laminated, it looked even worse. "I could be dead on a slab," I said, examining it closely.

My words hung in the air, suddenly seeming significant, and not just a throwaway line. I devoutly hoped I wasn't having a psychic flash. I'd never had one before, but there was always a first time.

He linked his fingers and looked blankly at me. I'd already noticed the calluses on his knuckles, evidence of long hours of practice in martial arts.

Giving him a severe look, I said, "You've missed your cue, Sid. You're supposed to be kind and assure me that my photo isn't a good likeness because in real life I'm quite good looking."

"It isn't a good likeness," he said. He paused, then went on, "I make it my business to know faces. I would recognize you anywhere, anytime, under any circumstances."

"I'm flattered," I said, "and I want you to know I feel the same about you. I'd go so far as to say you're unforgettable."

I worked at keeping my tone light, my body language relaxed. If Sid realized how much on edge I was, he'd wonder why, and I didn't want someone with his tenacity interested in ferreting out the reason for my anxiety.

He stood in one lithe movement. "No doubt you've heard of the telephone threat from those Australia's Redemption morons. I doubt they could swat a fly effectively, but I'm tightening security for everyone, just in case. From tomorrow, all vehicles will be searched when entering the car park area."

"You're not thinking someone would bring in a bomb!" I let my voice rise on the last word to a near squeak.

"Not knowingly, but it's child's play to break into a car and plant a device."

"Gosh."

"And be careful outside the Institute. You're in a hotel, aren't you?"

"Yes, the Windsor." Sid would not only know the hotel already, but probably my room number too.

"Don't open the door to anyone unless you check first. And look in the backseat of your car before you get into it."

I nodded, as concerned as Denise Brandt would be in the circumstances. "Sid, you don't think there's any *real* danger, do you?"

It was important to drop in his name. Like it or not — and I didn't — I had to forge some kind of amicable work relationship with him. For my part, I was going for an impression that blended respect with the casual friendliness of the girl-next-door variety. And what I hoped for in return was that Sid would dismiss me as a lightweight of no consequence.

He tucked the clipboard under his arm. "Probably not, but it's wise to take the necessary precautions." Reaching into the pocket of his black shirt, he pulled out a business card. "All staff have my number. I'm available night and day. If you see anything suspicious, call me. I'll get back to you fast, as all messages are forwarded to me wherever I am."

He left the office without waiting for my response, which was fortunate, since I wasn't sure what to say. "That's reassuring" seemed close to mockery, and "Thanks very much" was far too subservient.

Watching him walk down the hallway, I assessed his tightly muscled body and disciplined movements. He moved like a well-oiled killing machine, and I was unsettled by the realization that unless I had the element of total surprise, this was a guy I had no chance of besting in a physical encounter. Most men discount women in a conflict situation, but I had the feeling Sid Warde would be on full guard against any possible adversary, man, woman or child.

By the end of the day I was a shadow of the Denise who had hurried into work that morning. There was no way I had the energy to go looking for accommodations, so before I left the office I called and left a message at the accommodations bureau that I'd be in touch in the next day or so.

Joining a clump of other employees waiting at the lifts, I listened to the lighthearted chatter and wondered what thoughts went on behind those normal, pleasant faces. Each one of them had been vetted by the Institute to make sure he or she had the requisite convictions. Everyone standing here with me must despise races other than Caucasian, and desire to turn Australia into an all-white country. At some Hiddwing meetings I'd even heard discussed the lunatic idea that the Aborigines, our indigenous people, should be sent back to Asia, as eons ago they'd used a now-sunken landbridge to reach Australia.

When the lift stopped at the ground floor I looked for Jeffrey, but only Will Hiddwing got in. He was obviously popular with the staff, as several jocular comments were thrown his way. He grinned at me, little-boy style. "How's your first day been, Denise?"

"Pretty hectic."

"So I heard." He got out at the first level of parking, where the parking spots were bigger and the lighting seemed brighter. I wondered idly what I'd have to do if I wanted such superior parking — or rather, *who* I'd have to do. This made me grin.

"Will *is* nice," said Crystal, mistaking the reason for my smile.

Next to her Debbie, my other assistant, rolled her prominent brown eyes. "Crystal's keen on him," she announced to the occupants of the lift. Crystal reddened at the good-natured ribbing that followed this remark.

Two more stops followed before we were disgorged into the bowels of the underground parking. Calling a good-night to those unlucky enough to share the bottom level with me, I traipsed over to my rental car. I'd have to do something about buying a vehicle, because unless I did, it would give the impression I might not be intending to stay.

Hunger drove me to a McDonald's. It was crowded with other people seeking the comfort of high-fat, high-calorie food. My taste buds must have been tired too, as I didn't really remember eating the hamburger and fries I ordered. I took a long swallow of my Coke and looked around at the other tables. The noise level was high, and in a not unrelated fact, so was the number of kids ricocheting around.

I reassured myself yet again that it was unlikely but still possible that I'd been watched from the time I got off the plane from Melbourne. Now I was searching for a familiar face, a turn of the head or a gesture that had been picked up by my subconscious. There was nothing to set off a mental alarm. No one got up and followed me when I left the restaurant. No car pulled in behind me as I turned into the traffic. Of course, if Sid had anything to do with it, the surveillance would be expert, and I wouldn't see either of those things.

The anonymous hotel room was almost starting to feel like home. I had a fleeting pang when I thought of the familiar comfort of my own place, with my music, my books — and particularly my blue-and-white bathroom with its hanging ferns. It was a pleasure to clean one's teeth in such a room whilst looking out through the etched glass window at the mini forest I'd planted in the backyard. It was easy to visualize the bird feeders hanging in the trees, the truly amazing cast-iron birdbath that was almost as high as I was . . .

I shook myself. It was time to concentrate on the task at hand. After a rapid shower I changed into jeans and a dark T-shirt and sauntered through the hotel lobby with the manner of someone with time to kill. I strolled out into the warm early evening and set off toward the glowing neon lights of a movie complex just a few blocks away. Before I'd arrived I'd spent some time studying the immediate area surrounding the hotel on detailed maps, and yesterday, before I'd gone to the Institute, I'd walked the streets and wandered through the shops.

At the complex I glanced with apparent interest at the movies showing, but I was only really concerned with buying a ticket for the title that was showing in the theater situated close to an emergency exit that opened into a narrow alley running behind the building.

There weren't a lot of patrons at this early evening showing, so I had my choice of seats. Choosing one on the aisle halfway down, I waited until the theater darkened and the trailers for coming attractions began. As I got up to shift seats farther toward the back, I wondered why it was that the sound on movie trailers was always so deafening. I was watching to see if anyone else moved, but there were just a few latecomers hesitating in the darkness as they came through the curtains at the back.

After five minutes, I got up and left the theater. A couple of people followed me out — a man and a woman, who seemed not to be together — but maybe they were just interested in popcorn too.

Chomping on hot, buttery popcorn, I returned to the theater, this time sitting only a couple of rows from the back. After a pause, the two people who'd left with me returned, both with food of some sort. They moved farther down the theater and sat separately. This didn't mean much, as they could still be working together.

The main feature was beginning with a blare of self-important orchestral music. Feeling real regret, as I was enjoying the popcorn, I put the container under my seat, and, waiting for an opportune point when the screen went dark for a moment or two, I left for the second time, slipping quickly to the left and through the door marked EMERGENCY FIRE EXIT ONLY. During my explorations yesterday I'd checked out the movie complex and had experimentally opened the door, so I knew that doing so would not set off an alarm.

The door clicked shut behind me. The alley was deserted and surprisingly clean and well-lit. I hurried along, keeping to the center to guard against anyone lurking in a doorway. No one was. One block down I dodged into an intersecting alleyway, and halfway down that, I walked confidently through the rear employee entrance of an old, historic pub.

It had always fascinated me how looking as though you had every right to be somewhere seemed to automatically convince people that you did have that right. No one even glanced at me as I went past the staff locker rooms and trotted up a flight of stairs and into the main part of the pub.

It was charming, in a sort of rundown way, with old posters for beer and spirits featured on the dark walls and many small tables with spindly chairs. Jazz was playing loudly, two television sets, one above each end of the long bar, were blaring, and the crowd, though sparse, was already getting raucous.

The rest rooms were down a short hallway. The door to the men's side said BLOKES, the door to the women's SHEILAS. Just inside SHEILAS was a powder room with mirrors and, in one corner, a public telephone set in a little alcove. No one had been using it when I'd checked that it worked yesterday, and I was in luck again, as no one was using it now.

I jammed myself on the cramped little seat, sitting so that I could check anyone entering. As only a woman could come in here, if I was under surveillance by a man, it was just too bad for him.

"I'm pleased you've called," said Myra. There was a slight note of strain in her voice that prickled my skin. "We've got a lot to cover. First, we're activating Keeper. You okay with that?"

Keeper was code for Colin Lonie, who'd been set up as a close-position backup, to be called in if the assignment became more hazardous. The Hiddwing Institute used an outside firm, Upkeep Incorporated, to handle cleaning and maintenance in their buildings, and Colin had an employee record already in place with the company. It had been meticulously prepared, as the Institute insisted on its own security checks for anyone who had access to Hiddwing properties.

"Sure," I said, "but is it necessary?"

"Absolutely."

That one word told me things were escalating. There were ASIO agents I could access in Brisbane in an emergency, but Colin would be physically much closer to me on a day-to-day basis.

"Details?" I said, then, "Hold."

A large, rumpled woman had barged through the door. She looked at me with unfocused eyes, and mumbled, "The ladies?"

I pointed. "That way." I watched her lurch off in the direction of the toilets, then said to Myra, "Okay, go on."

Myra gave me the details of an appearance Rhys Hiddwing had made two months ago where it would have been possible for me to have been in the audience. "Don't beat him over the head with it," she said. "Introduce it into the conversation when an opportunity arises."

"You don't think I can be subtle, do you?"

Myra laughed. "You can try." I could picture her spiky hair and the grin on her expressive face.

All amusement disappeared from her voice as she went on to give me a rapid update of the progress in the investigation, interrupted by several exits and entrances into the SHEILAS. I checked everyone out as best I could from my vantage point in the corner, but saw no one even vaguely familiar.

The prime minister's condition was more than grave — he was almost certainly dying. The perpetrators had, as the news reported, refused to give any information, but ASIO had identified the woman as Tania Adalian, a member of an obscure Tasmanian extremist group with links to several like-thinking American organizations. For the moment, this information was under wraps.

Myra added, "We're investigating a report that Rosella and this woman have been linked in the past."

Rosella, I reminded myself, was Becky Hiddwing. "Linked how?"

"Sexually."

The fragmentary images the media had caught of the prime minister's shooting had shown only blurred impressions of the assailants, who had then melted into the crowd, and to the media's chagrin, no footage existed of the arrest of the suspects, or, indeed, of their transfer to the nearest secure confinement. I needed to know everything about Tania Adalian. "Can you get a photo and details to me?"

"On the way with Keeper."

We covered a few more logistical fine points, then it was my turn to give my information. I told her about the offer of a room at Jeffrey's house and how

I was being pressured to take it. "I'll get back to you on that," Myra said, "but I'm inclined to tell you to move in."

"Even though people mysteriously disappear?"

"Meaning?"

I gave her Vonny Quigley's name, the approximate date she'd last been seen, and the odd circumstances of her leaving. "Okay, I'm on that. Anything else?"

"One of the guests of honor last night was Lawrence Erman. I'll mail you any other names of interest to the dead-drop post office box, but I did think you'd want to know that a judge of the high court is a supporter."

"Indeed," said Myra. "I don't think intelligence has picked up that fact before. Perhaps he's a new convert."

She sounded even more surprised when I told her that Australia's Redemption had phoned in a threat to the Hiddwings' house the night before. "Hold on."

I heard muffled voices and the click of keyboard keys. Myra came back on the line to say, "We've been covering all the Hiddwing phones, both landline and cellular, for several months. A quick check of last night's transcripts doesn't show a threatening call from any group."

"No?"

"No. And Australia's Redemption is defunct. Our latest intelligence shows it doesn't exist any more."

"Oh."

"Yes, *oh*," said Myra.

CHAPTER NINE

I was on my own until Colin Lonie was transferred to the Hiddwing buildings' maintenance crew, so I used the time to settle in and make myself part of the team. I spent Wednesday and Thursday working hard and smiling a lot, and by the end of the week I was pretty much on easy terms with everyone I ran into during the course of my job. Kev the security guard greeted me whenever I was near the front door. Jeffrey constantly tried to lure me to the reception desk because, he said, I was the most entertaining person in the place, and he'd been touchingly pleased when I'd said I'd have a look at his house during the weekend to see if I'd consider moving in.

I'd even thawed Ed, the cantankerous guy in the booth at the parking entrance. This was well worth the effort, because who better to know the comings and goings of everyone in the building?

The Hiddwings hadn't been much in evidence. Rhys and Becky had been busy with interviews and appearances, although the tempo was dying down as the prime minister's condition was unchanged and the identities and motives of the would-be assassins remained unknown. I was ready with the "Oh, by the way, I've remembered where you might have seen me" story, but had had no opportunity to slip it into the conversation so far. In fact, if it hadn't been for Sid Warde, I probably wouldn't have bothered to cover this point. Rhys seemed to have forgotten the issue altogether.

In the last two days I'd become particularly friendly with Will Hiddwing, who, to Crystal's ill-concealed delight, had begun to drop into my office for brief chats.

"Will lives upstairs," she confided in me.

"Here, in the Institute?"

"There's a little apartment at the very top of the building. I've been in it!"

I'd looked suitably impressed. "Have you?"

Crystal giggled. "Just to take some things up to him when he had the flu. Not for anything else." Her voice indicated regret that this was the situation.

Friday morning I was lounging behind my desk, watching a TV news bulletin and eating a chocolate doughnut thoughtfully supplied by the management, when Will put his sandy head around the door.

"Busy?"

"Not at the moment."

He came in and plopped his light frame into a chair, giving a theatrical sigh as he did so. I thought again how unlike the standard-issue Hiddwing he was. Will had neither his father's presence nor his energy, and, although pleasant, he didn't have his aunt's formidable charm either. I wondered if his pliable, soft nature was a disappointment to his hard-driving father.

"I'm beat," Will said. "Making all these arrangements for a memorial service in the middle of nowhere is no joke, I can tell you."

"What memorial service?"

He yawned. "You'll hear all about it soon enough. It's seven years almost to the day that Oliver and Clara disappeared in the Outback, and my father thinks it's only fitting that there should be appropriate tributes paid to the founders of the Institute."

I took another bite of my doughnut. Delicious, fattening, and impossible to resist, especially when an assortment was delivered fresh every morning to the staff lunchroom. It would, I'd persuaded myself, be churlish to refuse such largesse from my employers. I swallowed, then said, "There's legal action pending to have them declared officially dead, isn't there?"

"It'll free up millions, held in trust. Dad can hardly wait."

I grinned at him. "That keen, eh?"

"He and Becky have got big plans for the Institute." He waved at the ceiling. "Sky's the limit."

"And what do you think?"

His mild expression changed subtly. "I don't think anything in particular."

"So this means there's going to be an expansion of activities?"

"And then some."

From his tone I knew I hadn't been mistaken. It was clear that Will Hiddwing had some reservations. "What would you do with the money if you had the only say about how it was used?"

"Me?" He gave a sharp laugh. "No one asks my opinion, so I don't give it."

I shook my head, commiserating. "I find your father and Becky do have rather overwhelming personalities."

He straightened in his chair, giving me an oh-come-now look. "Denise, I'd say it would be close to impossible to overwhelm you." He slumped his shoulders again. "And anyway, you're a professional, so they listen to you."

Just how disaffected are you?

I said, choosing my words with care, "It's one of the problems about working in a family business. I think it's often hard to get the credit you deserve."

Will was amused. "Family business? You make it sound like the Mafia."

"I didn't mean —"

"Hey, that's all right. It *is* a bit like the Mafia in some ways — you've got to toe the line, believe what you're supposed to believe." He pursed his lips, as though considering whether he'd go on, then said,

"That's why I like you, Denise. You don't keep preaching about it, like it's a religion or something. I mean, once Ilka starts, my eyes roll up in my head."

I was thinking how to play this promising situation when a voice came from the doorway. "Denise, I thought you'd like to see some clippings from the interstate papers."

I cursed to myself as Crystal undulated through the door, her eyes on Will. She'd obviously caught sight of him and manufactured an excuse to come into my office. She stopped in front of my desk, striking a pose with one hip out. "Hi, Will."

"Hi, Crystal." Will stood up. "Denise treating you well? I hear she's a bit of a slave-driver."

"She's all right." Crystal registered my raised eyebrows, and added hastily, "Like, better than all right . . . Um . . ."

"*Superb?*" I suggested. "Is that the word you're looking for?"

"I don't think so."

"Pity," I said, "you had a career ahead of you."

Will laughed, and Crystal gave me an uncertain smile. "Like you're joking, right?" she said.

"Like I'm joking."

Will sauntered to the door, hands in pockets. "Love to stay and talk to you two, but I suppose I'd better get back to work." He turned back to say, "I nearly forgot the reason I was here in the first place. Dad wants to know if you're free for dinner tomorrow night." He grinned mischievously. "Or maybe you've got a heavy date?"

"I'm not quite into the Brisbane social whirl yet," I said. "But it's only a matter of time until I make the social pages."

"So that's a yes?"

"I'd be delighted."

"Okay, seven-thirty for drinks. Dinner at eight. Helena and a couple of others will be there, so dress up a bit. Want me to pick you up?"

Crystal frowned.

"I'll drive myself, thanks. I'm sure I can find the way."

Crystal's face cleared slightly. "Jeffrey's got a map," she offered. "I'll go down with you, Will, and collect one for Denise."

I didn't need a map, but who was I to stand in the way of budding romance? "Great," I said, suddenly distracted by the sight of Colin Lonie, dressed in khaki overalls, stepping out of the lift. It was one of the advantages of being in a glass-walled fish bowl that you could see people approaching. A disadvantage, of course, was that everything you did was in plain view.

I hoped my face had registered nothing. I said to Will, "Please thank Rhys for the invitation. Is something specific being discussed? Do I need to prepare anything beforehand?"

He almost pouted. "The same old topics will get a beating. You can wing it. You know all that stuff already."

From my point of view, resentment was good to see in someone who might, for that reason, be a source of valuable information. I sent a silent apology to Crystal, because, although I wasn't the slightest interested in Will Hiddwing at any deep personal level, if necessary, I would make him think I was.

"You know," I said, "can I change my mind? I would like a lift tomorrow night."

* * * * *

Colin was making a circuit of the offices in the company of Fred Nesbitt, the owner of Upkeep Incorporated. I'd met Fred earlier. He was a nuggety, bowlegged little guy with the handshake of a professional wrestler and a sort of aggressive friendliness that had him referring to everyone, male or female, as "mate."

"How are you, mate?" he said, stepping into my office with Colin in tow. He checked his clipboard, probably to make sure he knew my name.

"I'm just great, Fred."

"Good news, mate. Now, this is Col, right? He'll be doing maintenance in the building, and I'm showing him the ropes."

The photo ID on Colin's chest depicted the same impassive expression with which Col was regarding me now. I said brightly, "Hi, Col."

He nodded slowly. "Hi."

Twisting my head around, I glared at the ceiling. "Fred, while Col's here he can fix that outlet up there. The draft from the air conditioning's giving me a stiff neck."

Fred didn't seem pleased. "You haven't filled out a form."

"Oh, mate," I said, contrite. "You know how things have been around here over the last few days. And being new, I wasn't quite sure of the correct procedure."

Fred grunted, but the "mate" had won him over. "Okay," he said, "we'll skip the red tape this time. I'll send Col back when we've finished our tour of the place."

In half an hour Colin was back, carrying a bag of tools and a step ladder. He knocked on the frame of the door. "Excuse me? It's Col, here to fix the vent."

There wasn't a glimmer of humor on his face, and I felt a warm glow of admiration. Colin and I had trained together, and I knew him to be irrepressibly funny, but no trace of his true personality showed. He was colorless, not-very-bright Col, the maintenance man.

I moved from behind the desk to let him set up the stepladder. Before he mounted it, he fished in his pocket. "Paperwork," he said, handing me roughly folded pages. "You have to sign the work order, Fred says. And if I use any materials, you have to initial a requisition order." He frowned at me. "I think I've got that right."

"Are you going to be long?"

Colin gave me a perfect tradesperson long-suffering look. "Long as it takes, lady."

Muttering, I took a pile of papers from my desk and plopped down in a chair as far from this activity as possible. Although it was entirely likely that surveillance cameras were trained on the offices — I could just picture Sid poring over the multiple screens in his command center — I hadn't been able to spot any telltale lens. Nevertheless, it was necessary to act as though I were being watched, so I palmed the small folded insert between the pages he'd handed me, and then made a good show of impatiently scanning, and then signing, the work order.

Colin made an equally good show of fixing the vent. "There you go," he said, clambering down from the ladder. "She's apples now, I'd say."

"Thanks," I said, offhand, passing him the signed work order.

"Here's my pager number," he said, "in case there's still a problem with the air."

I squinted in the direction of the vent. "You mean you haven't fixed it?"

"Done the best I can."

I didn't look at him as he gathered up his tools and left the office, because to me he had to be just a guy in overalls who was on call to fix things in the building, and not Keeper, my backup and lifeline if anything went really wrong.

Working for Fred Nesbitt's Upkeep Incorporated, Colin's responsibilities included both the Institute office building and the estate, so he was in a position to manufacture convincing reasons to enter either of them at short notice.

My phone rang. I picked it up at once — PR point: Never let a phone ring more than twice. "Denise Brandt," I said with crisp competency.

Rhys Hiddwing's urgent voice said, "Please come to my office immediately."

Ilka was waiting for me at the entrance to the executive suites. "What's up?" I said.

She compressed her lips into a thin line and shook her head.

"Your lips are sealed, Ilka?"

"It is better for Rhys to tell you."

Intrigued, I hurried to keep up with her. "Hey, slow down. Is something wrong?"

She shot me an exasperated look over her shoulder.

"You have no patience." To my astonishment, her face crumpled a little. "It is . . . disturbing news."

Becky, her expression somber, was in her brother's office. "Denise, sit down. Something unexpected has happened."

Nothing in either Rhys or Becky's manner suggested they were about to accuse me of being an undercover ASIO agent, so I was interested, but not alarmed. "It is something I can help with?"

"Almost certainly," said Rhys. "When the news gets out, the media will come baying after us again."

I sat up, alert and suitably grave. "It's serious then?"

Rhys ran his hands through his red hair, the plain wedding ring on his left hand catching the light. "A body's been found." He glanced at his sister, then back at me. "Or rather, what's left of a body after seven years."

I looked from brother to sister. Rhys seemed by far the more shocked of the two. Glancing up at Ilka, I was surprised to see a sheen of tears in her eyes.

Becky said, "We were contacted this morning. Naturalists in the Outback near the Queensland border were canvassing an area around a remote waterhole. From certain things scattered in the area . . ."

"Our father," said Rhys. "After all these years, someone's stumbled across what's left of our father."

105

CHAPTER TEN

I was on call in case the finding of what was left of Oliver Hiddwing blew up into a big story, but the only mention I saw was a small paragraph in the morning paper saying that a skull and other skeletal remains of an as-yet-unidentified person had been discovered by a scientific party surveying a remote desert area.

The Hiddwings had pulled strings and a rush DNA analysis was being performed, so within a few days the family would know for sure if it was Oliver

Hiddwing who'd been found. Once that news leaked out, a media storm was a given.

For the moment all was quiet on the PR front, so that meant that after I completed two chores, the rest of my Saturday was free, at least until the evening. First stop was Jeffrey's house. Myra had noted in the material Colin had given me that she thought I should move in, although the decision was mine. She believed it was worth the slight extra risk of detection, considering the information I might gain in casual conversation from the other employees of the Institute. After I'd given the place the once-over, I'd have the final say.

The place Jeffrey was renting was about a kilometer from the Institute and situated on a neat, tree-lined street. I drove up the steep hill and parked outside an old Queensland colonial-style house. It was delightful: Set on tall poles with a lattice skirt for modesty, it had wide verandas on each side and was topped with a red tin roof. Painted deep cream with russet doors and trim, it seemed serenely at home in a row of similar homes.

Before I was up the wooden steps the door opened and Jeffrey appeared. His massive thighs stretched the material of his shorts, and his chest seemed about to burst out of his tattered T-shirt.

"This is great," he said, smiling. "Come on in." It was warming to be received with such unalloyed pleasure.

"The outside's lovely," I said in appreciation.

He stood aside to usher me past him like a proud parent about to show off photogenic offspring. "The inside's freshly painted too."

I admired the entrance hall, the walls, and ceiling, which were still the original painted wooden boards.

"Hi," said a guy wearing shorts, thongs, and a day's worth of stubble. He was sprawled along a sofa in the front room with pages of a racing form guide spread around. He was in the process of making red marks to indicate his selections.

"Sam works in training," said Jeffrey, grinning, "and he's used to telling everyone what to do, but it doesn't help him much with the ponies."

Jeffrey led the way down the hall toward the back of the house. "Let's start in the kitchen." Over his shoulder he said, "Sorry you can't meet Charlotte, but she's away for the weekend with Sid."

"Not Sid Warde?"

"Yeah, that's right. They've been an item for months. Quite serious, I think."

I hadn't planned to be this close to Sid outside work, but I'd make the best of it and make sure that Charlotte found me pleasant, uncomplicated, and unremarkable, as I was sure Sid would ask her about me.

Jeffrey continued to show me the good features — apparently there were no bad — of the house. It was automatic for me to check the security of doors and windows and map out escape routes, and I thought I was being unobtrusive until Jeffrey shocked me by saying, "Looking for escape routes, eh?"

"Pardon?"

He patted my shoulder in approval. "You're a girl after my own heart. I do the same as you, everywhere I go. You can't know when there'll be a fire or an earthquake or whatever. Scope it out, be prepared, and you'll survive, I always say." He pointed to the wall in the kitchen where a circular device was attached near the ceiling, its red eye shining to show it was alive. "Smoke alarm. Same in every room. And carbon monoxide testers. Got them too. And I'll show you where the extinguishers are."

His tour of the house ended up in the room Vonny Quigley had rented from Jeffrey. Several cardboard cartons were stacked on a colored mat. On top of them was a small pile of envelopes, held with a rubber band.

Jeffrey saw me looking at them. "I wasn't quite sure what to do with Vonny's mail because I thought she might call and give her new address. Looks like they're mostly bills, so I suppose I should return them and say she isn't here any longer."

I felt a chill, as though these few possessions and untouched mail was all that was left of her.

Myra's notes had included the brief comment that Veronica Quigley hadn't been officially reported as a missing person, perhaps not surprising because, as Jeffrey had said earlier, she appeared to have no living relatives. She had neither used her credit cards nor accessed her bank accounts in the last five weeks. She had, to all intents and purposes, vanished into thin air.

Jeffrey patted the nearest carton. "I'll find somewhere under the house for these." He looked at me hopefully. "You could move in straightaway if you wanted."

I went over to the window. We were set up so high

that there was a wonderful view over a valley of red roofs and burgeoning greenery. I was sure birds would wake every morning with enthusiastic choruses.

"I'm awfully flattered, Jeffrey, but why are you so keen to have me here?"

He seemed abashed. "Well, I like you a lot, and all that, but jeez, I got a lot of rent to pay, and having one more person will really make the difference."

"I'm not so flattered now," I said.

He made a face at me. "So what do you think?"

"I'll move in tomorrow."

Leaving Jeffrey a pleased man, I set off for my second chore of the day, a meeting with Elise. Yesterday she'd been called into Rhys's office while I was still there and told about the discovery in the desert. Sooner or later — and probably sooner — the media would learn that Oliver Hiddwing's body had been found, and the fascinating fact that there was no sign at all of his sister Clara's remains.

Elise was to prepare material for the Web site that would address this issue as soon as it became public, and hopefully dampen some of the speculation that was guaranteed to erupt at the hint of mystery and the possibility of scandal in such a high-profile family.

To Elise's barely concealed fury, Becky had instructed her that I was to okay the text. She was to get it ready to go as soon as possible because there was no way of knowing when the news story would break.

Once we were both outside the executive suites,

Elise had made it very plain what she thought of the situation. "I won't have this written until tomorrow." Her look dared me to comment. "And I'm damned if I'm coming into the Institute over the weekend. I suppose it's too much to hope that you have a laptop so I can upload it to you?"

"I'm afraid I haven't got a laptop."

She sighed her irritation. "There's no way I can send sensitive stuff like this by fax to the hotel, so you can just come to my place tomorrow morning."

"Okay."

She ignored my agreeable reply, snapping, "And don't say it's too much trouble. I've got all the preparations for a dinner party Saturday night, and I've no intention of leaving the house."

"Just give me your address. I'll be there."

Elise glared at me. "This makes my job that much harder, you know."

"Sorry," I'd said. It was Becky Hiddwing whom Elise should be blaming, and of course Elise knew that, but it was clear she had no intention of complaining direct to the source of her anger.

Elise lived on the other side of Brisbane, so I checked my map at every red light, somehow finding my way in the right direction. Her house was in an old area that had a kind of slightly rundown charm, like a faintly disreputable relative who's seen better days. I found her street after driving in circles for a while and finally cracking and asking a guy at a service station for directions.

Her house suited the area well. The gardens were just a little neglected, the front porch sagged a trifle, the front door needed a touch of paint.

I rang the bell and waited, saying hello to a black cat who was curled up on an ancient chair on the porch. He gave me a pink, bored yawn. I was going to try to win him over, but at that moment Elise, swathed in a multicolored housecoat, snatched open the door. "It's you."

"It *is* me."

She gave me a grudging smile. "Oh, come in and have a drink or something. It's a bore to drive halfway across Brisbane in Saturday morning traffic."

Inside the house was just as I had pictured it, which amazed me. I was usually totally off the mark when I guessed what people's places would be like. The rooms were crammed with fussy furniture, throw cushions, knickknacks, a variety of candles — unlit at this stage, of course — and many framed photographs. There was a strong smell of incense mingled with dust.

Elise led the way out to the kitchen, which was just as crammed. Pots and pans hung in iron baskets, growing herbs overflowed their pots on the windowsill, the double sink was filled with bowls and saucepans, and every bit of counter space was taken up with containers, ingredients, and utensils.

"I'm up to my eyebrows, as you can see." She looked around at the chaos. "God, it's a bloody wonder I can get an edible meal out of this. That's what you're thinking, isn't it?"

"I was thinking you must be a gourmet cook."

My attempt at diplomacy amused Elise. "Oh yeah? I haven't poisoned anyone yet. That's the best I can say for myself."

Rummaging around in the breakfast nook, which was piled with newspapers and magazines, she extracted some pages. "Here you are. Want a coffee while you read it?"

Although somewhat dubious about her ancient coffee percolator, I said, "Why not?"

"You won't get better coffee," she declared, searching in a cupboard for a mug. I took a cautious sip and discovered to my astonishment she was right. "Hey," I said, "this is good."

"I'll try not be insulted by your surprise."

I grinned at her. "This stuff you've written is excellent, Elise. You know it is. And it's a total drag that Becky wants me to see it, because of course I'm not going to change anything. I only wish I could write as well."

The compliment was sincere, and Elise was placated. She grabbed another mug, poured herself coffee, topped up mine, and slid into the seat opposite me. "I shouldn't be angry," she said. "Becky does this all the time."

I made an encouraging go-on noise.

Elise looked at me with a serious expression. "Don't get sucked in," she said. "Becky takes a fancy to people, and it's great for them. Then . . ." She spread her hands.

"They're on the outer?" I suggested.

"You get the picture."

Seeing that Elise was in a receptive mood, I took the opportunity to say, "I need some advice."

"About what?" Like most people, she was pleased to be asked for her opinion.

"I'm thinking of moving into a room in Jeffrey's house, but I'm a bit worried about something. It seems I'm taking the place of someone called Vonny Quigley, who suddenly up and left."

"That's right, a month or so ago. She just didn't turn up for work one day."

I leaned forward confidentially. "I was wondering if maybe Jeffrey or the other guy, Sam, put the hard word on Vonny, if you see what I mean. I wouldn't want to move in if I was going to have to put up with something like that."

Elise laughed. "No way was that the situation. Besides, Jeffrey's having a romance with bodybuilding and hardly has time for the real thing."

The subject of Vonny was open, so I said, "Whatever did happen to her, do you think?"

Elise shrugged. "She was in research, mostly concentrating on overseas stuff. Anyway, Vonny was one of those quiet people — you know the sort. Watched and listened, but didn't say much. Secretive, too. Never said a thing about herself or what she did in her spare time."

"So why would she just go like that?"

"Jesus!" said Elise. "Look at the time!" She leapt to her feet. "Sorry, but I've got to get cracking. There're eight people coming tonight, and they're going to expect something spectacular."

As she ushered me out the door, she said, "About Vonny . . . I wouldn't give it another thought. I'm sure she left for some personal reason that had nothing to do with Jeffrey or anyone else at the Institute."

"Thanks for your advice," I said, looking appropriately grateful, although I didn't believe a word of it. I was convinced something lethal had happened to Vonny Quigley and that someone at the Institute knew all about it.

When I left Elise's I had no particular destination in mind. Ahead of me stretched several hours when I could be myself and not be on guard. A gorgeous green park by the river beckoned, and I did something Myra would have frowned at — worse, she would have ordered me not to do it. I called Roanna.

Adjacent to a kiosk selling drinks and ice cream I found a public telephone. I'd be exposed, but no one could get close to me without detection. Besides, why shouldn't Denise Brandt be calling a friend on an impulse, when out for a stroll on a warm summer Saturday?

I dialed Roanna's private number, wondering where on the island she'd be this time on Saturday. It was possible she'd been in the administration building, dealing with tourists' problems, or maybe sitting on her little private veranda, gazing through the tropical trees to blue-green water.

"Hello?" She sounded tentative, and that wasn't what I expected. It didn't go with her strong, tough persona.

"It's Denise. Can you talk?"

"Yes, I'm at home. Where are you?"

"Too far away."

I shouldn't have done this. I could visualize her face, her dark hair, the way she threw back her head when she laughed. A wave of longing engulfed me, so that my throat closed.

Roanna said, "Are you on a job?"

"Nothing I can discuss."

"Of course not." There was a pause and I could hear her breathing. "Am I going to see you?"

"Don't know when — but yes, of course you are."

I could be on a plane and in her arms by late this afternoon.

"Roanna, I . . ."

"Yes?"

"I miss you."

"Me too." She sighed. "You have no idea how much."

We spoke for a few more minutes, but it was a forced, unsatisfying conversation. I wanted to see her in person, to be there on Aylmer Island in the Whitsunday Passage, inside the embrace of the Great Barrier Reef. I promised to call again soon, and we broke the connection.

Brisbane seemed suddenly boring and flat. Even the passionfruit ice-cream cone I purchased didn't have the zing I anticipated. Wandering through the park, willing myself to enjoy the morning, I found myself unhappy and restless, and cursed myself for calling her. Roanna's voice at the end of a line would never be enough. I wanted much more, and to hell with regulations.

The first time we had kissed was as vivid to me as if it were yesterday. For the first time I'd actually understood what the old cliché *swept away on a tide of passion* meant. I'd been more than swept away; I'd been lifted to heights I'd never thought possible.

I sat on a bench near the water and brooded. Roanna wasn't under indictment, she'd never been arrested for any crime, so wasn't she just an ordinary citizen with whom I could have any relationship I wished? If it had only been as simple as that. Roanna hadn't been cleared in ASIO's eyes, just never charged because of lack of evidence. Myra would point out that ASIO regulations were strict about off-the-job personal relationships with people deemed possible security risks.

A small convoy of brown ducks spotted me and paddled over to investigate my possibilities. I tossed them bits of ice-cream cone and watched them vie for each fragment with feathery aggression.

It was no good sitting here moping, when tonight I'd face the Hiddwings at home. I'd need to be on my toes, ready for anything. I closed my eyes and reviewed the information Colin had passed to me yesterday. After I'd read it in my hotel room and committed everything to memory, I'd torn the thin pages into tiny pieces and flushed them down the toilet.

Along with the sparse details of her career and background that had been uncovered, there'd been a reproduction of Tania Adalian's image, seemingly taken from a photo at a social occasion. The prime minister's assailant was twenty-five but looked younger. She had a pixie-ish, mischievous face and a warm smile.

An only child, she'd had a middle-class upbringing in what seemed a perfectly normal family. She'd been a reasonable student and had gone on to study computer programming, working in the field without distinguishing herself in any particular way.

This was not the popular picture of a terrorist, but there was some evidence that she'd been at least peripherally involved in the bombing of an abortion clinic that had led to two deaths, as well as the torture murder of an outspoken environmentalist. She'd been questioned, but no charges had ever been brought. Mainly it was guilt by association, as she had socialized with members of a loosely linked group of like thinkers who apparently worked together at times on different terrorist projects.

Tania Adalian's connection with the Hiddwing Institute was only through Becky Hiddwing. They had had, by all reports, a brief, but torrid affair. Becky had showered her with gifts and they'd been, for a while, inseparable.

Then things had cooled. Tania had returned to her native Tasmania, and Becky, heart clearly unbroken, had started a romance with a male actor, who in turn had been replaced with someone else within a few months.

As for Tania Adalian's companion in the attempted assassination, he was still unidentified, and analysts had come to the conclusion that it was likely he was a lowly foot soldier, deployed like Tania Adalian as a loyal but expendable follower of a greater cause.

As a footnote, Myra had included information on Australia's Redemption. The driving force, a disaffected academic who had sucked a small number of students into his philosophical viewpoint, had died some months ago after driving drunk and crashing his car into an inconvenient tree. Headless, the group had fallen apart. So, unless a former member had taken the name of the group to use, Australia's Redemption could not have threatened the Hiddwings last Monday night.

Myra had written at the bottom of the page: *Excuse for heightened security? If so, why?*

It was a good question. Perhaps, like ripples from a dropped stone into a pond, whispers about surveillance by national security had spread, touching the Hiddwing shore. If that was so, then I was in danger, and so was Colin. We were recent additions to the Institute, and therefore more likely to be plants.

Or perhaps there was a simpler reason — the knowledge that the Hiddwing Institute and similar organizations would be targets for close attention because the people who had tried to kill the prime minister clearly shared the same anti-immigration views.

And of course, should the Hiddwings themselves be actively involved in the affair, there was every reason for them to want a tight control on everything that came in or went out of the Institute.

Quacking broke into my thoughts. Several ducks were squabbling over some delicacy in the water. I threw the last of my ice-cream cone in their direction, and they fought over that. Then, having correctly assessed me as having nothing further to offer, the little convoy set off for a new source of sustenance.

I watched them with the whimsical thought that I was like one of those ducks — gliding along on top while paddling furiously underneath.

CHAPTER ELEVEN

Will Hiddwing did not share Jeffrey's passion for punctuality. Fifteen minutes after the appointed time he roared up to the hotel's entrance in a new BMW. "Birthday present from Dad," he said as the doorman opened the passenger door for me.

It was the top-of-the-line model, dark blue with cream upholstery, and it still had that delightful new-car smell. "Pretty sensational," I said, sinking back in the leather seat. I smiled appreciatively at him, intending to set myself up as the perfect, lighthearted companion. My primary aim — well-disguised, I hoped — was to extract information.

It was a pity, but Will had no idea how to drive his BMW skillfully. He was one of those infuriating people who pay little attention to what is happening ahead on the road, so they accelerate too fast and then brake too hard. It was clear this trip was going to be a tiresome series of jerky transitions from fast to slow and back again.

Gritting my teeth, and entertaining the fantasy that maybe Will would offer to let me try the car out before my stomach rebelled and I was carsick, I said, "I've never driven this model, but I'd love to have a try . . ." I would have batted my eyelashes, but Will wasn't looking in my direction.

"Very responsive machine," he announced with the air of an expert. He slammed on the brakes, having suddenly registered that the traffic lights we'd been approaching had been red for some time. "Great braking system."

"I can see that," I said.

Will obviously didn't notice my dry tone, as he looked over at me to say, "You're looking very nice tonight."

"Thank you." I had taken trouble with my appearance, choosing a classically simple pale green dress, and adding only a wristwatch and plain gold stud earrings. "You look pretty good yourself."

He did. Will had the thin, flat-stomached frame that made his clothes look subtly elegant, and he'd gone for simplicity too: a white shirt, dark pants, and a loose, trendy jacket.

Not bothering with false modesty, Will said, "I'd

say it's a good thing Crystal isn't invited tonight. She wouldn't be able to keep her hands off me."

"The young have so little self-control," I observed. "But I'm surprised you're not flattered by the attention."

"Well, maybe I am — a bit." The traffic signal ahead of us had been green for several seconds, and when the car behind us tooted, Will stamped on the accelerator so hard that the BMW leapt forward as though kicked by a gigantic boot. He took his eyes off the road to say with a roguish grin, "I'd rather *you* were interested in me."

"Gosh," I said. "This is unexpected." Perhaps a girlish giggle would have been appropriate at this point, but I couldn't bring myself to do it.

"Of course," Will said in a sly tone, "I'd have to fight my aunt for you."

"Becky?"

"Only aunt I've got."

"I don't believe it."

Will snorted. "No? She's the one who insisted you be invited to dine with the wheelers and dealers tonight. And you've been at the Institute for how long? A week?"

"For many months, if you count Melbourne," I said with mock indignation.

Conflicting emotions filled me. If Will wasn't joking, then Becky's interest would put me close to a wonderful source of information right at the very top of the organization. But, on the other hand, this was a complication with which I really didn't want to deal. Before I was deployed in the field, Myra had suggested this very thing as an outside possibility, and I remembered how I'd mocked the whole idea of Becky

Hiddwing taking a sexual interest in me. I recalled I'd laughed and said to Myra, "Are you telling me I should give my all for my country?"

"That's your decision," Myra had replied, without even the trace of a smile.

My attention was jolted back to the present as Will braked and swore at an inoffensive little sedan that had dared to turn onto the road from a side street. I glanced over at his furious face. At work Will gave the impression of being Mr. Mild, and this was a side of him I hadn't suspected existed.

Once he'd roared past the other vehicle, and in his own mind put the middle-aged guy in his place, Will's usual pleasant expression returned. He said, "I know that Becky asked Sid to take a look at your personal life."

"I haven't got much of a private life," I said. "Heart broken, all that stuff, long ago."

Will chuckled. "I don't think it's your heart Becky's interested in."

The ASIO background that had been constructed for me painted Denise Brandt as largely uninvolved, with no close friends to speak of and little in the way of romantic entanglements. As her records showed that she had spent a lot of time working overseas, it hadn't been deemed necessary to invent any boyfriends, or for that matter, girlfriends. Denise Brandt was, to all intents and purposes, exactly what she claimed to be — a loner, and an asexual loner at that.

There was a break in our conversation while Will got into a shouting match with a guy in a large Mercedes who had tried to change lanes just as Will had made one of his periodic hard accelerations.

When things had calmed down, I changed the

subject to one I'd made a mental note to pursue. Will had been eighteen when Oliver and Clara Hiddwing disappeared. "What were they like, your grandfather and great-aunt?"

Will looked over at me. "It was seven years ago."

"You're telling me your memories have faded with time?"

He laughed. "Indelible personalities, both of them. Couldn't forget them if I tried." He paused, then went on in a serious tone. "Grandfather was formidable — deep voice, piecing eyes, the works. That said, it was Aunt Clara who really made you jump. She could just say something, quietly, no emphasis — and everyone ran to do whatever she suggested."

"Your father too?"

"He was her favorite, actually. I always noticed how her voice softened when she talked to him. It wasn't fair, because she scared the hell out of everyone else, but he had a charmed life where she was concerned."

"So I suppose he's particularly upset, since only your grandfather's body has been found. He must be wondering what happened to Clara Hiddwing."

"We're *all* wondering what happened to Aunt Clara. You know, I wouldn't put it past her to still be alive somewhere."

"You're kidding."

He smiled at my incredulous tone. "Of course I'm kidding. I'd say what's left of her is out there too, near where Grandfather was found, although Aunt Clara was as hard as nails. It's hard to imagine any harsh conditions that could kill her."

"What were they doing there in that remote area?

I heard it was some sort of survival trek or something, but hell, they weren't young, were they?" When he frowned at this, I added hastily, "I know they were both very fit, but the conditions must have been almost unendurable."

"It's a Hiddwing tradition," said Will, his tone sardonic. "Any true Hiddwing likes to be tested to the max. We're supposed to be physically, mentally, and emotionally superior." His mouth twisted in a bitter smile. "Surely you knew that?"

"Sounds like hard work," I said.

"You're going to be finding out how hard," said Will. "Dad's decided to change the next staff wilderness retreat to the Outback, near where Oliver and Clara disappeared."

This was madness, as searing temperatures in Australia's desert heart were standard for this time of year. "But it's summer, Will. It'll be like a furnace out there."

"Tell me about it. Of course, such things aren't supposed to worry the Hiddwings. And too bad about everyone else."

I wasn't happy. The original wilderness destination had been a remote rain forest area, and I'd been looking forward to the excursion. Fiery red desert terrain was not on my list of must-sees. "Do I have to go?"

Will grunted. "If I tried to get out of it, and failed miserably, you certainly have no hopes of a reprieve. Of course, some members of staff will be gung-ho to demonstrate how super fit they are."

"I suppose you mean Jeffrey."

"Jeffrey? No — I meant bloody Ilka."

It seemed Ilka's scorn for Will was returned with interest. "Ilka likes hiking in the desert?" I said, visualizing her cool blond self. "I don't believe it."

"To impress my father, she'll do anything." He thumped the horn as the vehicle ahead of us slowed to turn off on a side road. In a caustic tone he added, "She'd be my stepmother, if she could."

"She's got her sights set on Rhys?"

"Too right, she has. And she knows I don't like it."

I let a few moments pass before I said, "Ilka didn't ever meet your grandfather, did she?"

He turned his head sharply. "She came to the Institute a couple of years after he disappeared. What's that got to do with anything, anyway?"

"It's just that Ilka was there when Rhys gave me the news about the discovery of the remains, and she seemed upset."

Will made a sound of disgust. "That's to impress Dad that she really *cares*."

The ASIO intelligence report on Ilka Britten showed a ruthless, driven woman with no suggestion of a tender side. But hey, even Hitler had loved dogs. "If Ilka doesn't really care, why is she interested in your father?"

Impatient, Will shook his head. "The bitch gets off on power."

I thought he was selling Ilka short. On Monday at the party, her longing expression when she had looked after the departing Rhys had stuck me as completely genuine, as had her jealousy when she thought there was any possibility that I might be a rival.

He looked over at me, his expression sour. "After all the preparatory stuff I've done, Ilka takes great pleasure in waltzing in on Friday to tell me the whole blasted memorial service is now on hold."

His attention wasn't on the road, and we began to drift toward the verge. "We're running off the edge," I said, ever helpful.

"What?" He wrenched the wheel, his face furious. "It's the camber of the road."

It was clear that Will didn't take kindly to any criticism of his driving, especially when the subject of Ilka had already upset him. In a voice of calm sanity, I said soothingly, "But your work won't go to waste, will it? The memorial service changes a little and becomes a funeral. I mean, they're not that much different, are they?"

"You don't seem to realize the predicament we're in," he snapped. "They've found the family patriarch, but no accompanying matriarch."

A trite comment seemed appropriate, so I said, "I'm sure she'll be located soon."

"She better be. I mean, the cops are involved, would you believe? And God knows where that will lead."

"It's standard when there's an unexplained death. The police have to find evidence to present at the inquest."

"Jesus Christ," he said, "some cop turned up at the estate this morning to interview my father. I don't know what the guy said, but Dad looked like death after he left."

Pre-dinner drinks were served in the same room where I had first met Becky Hiddwing. Sipping French champagne, I glanced at the portrait above the fireplace, then at the real woman. The painting was flattering, but then, the artist had had excellent bone structure and appealing coloring with which to work. Tonight her auburn hair was brushed back from her face, emphasizing that excellent bone structure. She wore a red dress that should have clashed with her hair, but somehow didn't, and a single diamond at her throat.

She had looked up when Will and I entered the room, and sent me a quick, intimate smile. I told myself Becky's charm was synthetic, but I couldn't help being pleased at the personal attention.

There were seven of us for dinner. The Institute was represented by Rhys, Becky, and Will — and me. The guests were Gustave Zeeman, rising politician, Axel Dorca, risen entrepreneur, and Helena Court-Howerd, power broker. I wondered why Ilka hadn't been invited.

Beside me, Will picked up on my thought. "No Ilka, you notice," he said. "I suppose it's too much to hope she's falling out of favor."

"Denise, you're the only person who hasn't met everyone," said Becky, slipping her hand under my elbow. "Let me do the honors." In a softer voice she added, "You're looking great."

Helena Court-Howerd favored me with a chilly smile. "We've met." She paused to suck in her already hollow cheeks as Will bent to light the cigarette in her long holder. "We were discussing your scruples, or some such, I believe."

I had to admire her recall. "Yes, it was just before the news about the prime minister."

Helena's eyes narrowed. "Ah yes, the Honorable Albert Paggi. I hear by the grapevine that he's not long for this world, and good riddance." She blew out a plume of smoke and added viciously, "Wishy-washy bleeding heart."

Becky laughed. "And what do you really think of him, Helena?"

Helena apparently didn't see the joke. "I've no time for anyone who sells Australia out to foreigners," she said, delivering the last word with whiplash emphasis.

"Denise and I have met before too," announced Axel Dorca, lifting his heels so he was a little taller. He was gazing up at me with such exaggerated enthusiasm that I decided there and then that he was possibly gay, and in the severest of denials.

"Still lonely?" he asked.

"I'm afraid I wasn't in the first place."

Dorca reached into his breast pocket, then with a flourish presented me with his business card. "If you *do* get lonely," he said, "you can call me any time."

Becky steered me on to a man who was deep in conversation with Rhys. "Gustave, this is Denise Brandt, who's now running our PR department."

Zeeman turned toward me, his open, boyish face registering a pleasant enthusiasm. I was keen to meet Gustave Zeeman in the flesh, having seen him on television many times. He was a little shorter than I'd expected, but radiated the good-natured fellowship that made him so dangerous. He was a natural politician, polished and convincing, and able to make almost anything seem eminently reasonable. He could sugarcoat the most extreme stance, delivering a racist, noninclusive message in such nonthreatening, soothing words that the poison slipped unnoticed into receptive minds.

What was even more disquieting was the speed with which Zeeman's star had risen, greatly helped by Helena Court-Howerd's support. And recently pundits had begun discussing his future as a possible leader of the country.

Zeeman took my right hand in both of his and pumped it gently as he gazed warmly into my eyes. "I am so pleased to meet you," he said with convincing sincerity.

"Because you've heard so much about me?"

Zeeman stopped pumping and looked at me oddly. "Well, no . . ." He recovered to add, "But I'm sure every report would be excellent."

"Denise is our newest addition to the Institute family," said Rhys. "And in many ways one of the best." His voice had none of its usual resonance. Will had been right: Rhys Hiddwing looked physically ill.

Zeeman favored me with a charming smile. "I'm sure that Rhys and Becky are delighted to have your expertise."

A woman, all in black, came to the door to announce that dinner was served. She reminded me irresistibly of Mrs. Danvers in *Rebecca,* and I had a fleeting image of this whole ugly building going up in flames while, artistically backlit by the fire, she stood at an upstairs window. I repressed a smile: Myra had been right about my vivid imagination.

We dined in a small room hung with heavy maroon drapes and furnished with equally heavy dark furniture. The table was massive and the individual chairs both unsightly and uncomfortable. Rhys sat at one end and Becky at the other. I found myself between Rhys, who was somber and uncommunicative, and Gustave Zeeman, who was ebullient and talkative. I chatted with Zeeman in an artless fashion while keeping my ears tuned for anything interesting happening elsewhere at the table.

The food was good but unremarkable, and the conversations seemed about the same. That is, until Helena Court-Howerd said in her penetrating voice, "Rhys, I've heard a very distressing rumor through my source in the police commissioner's office. Perhaps you might set the record straight."

Everyone stopped talking. Becky said, "Rhys?" in a cautionary tone, but he shook his head at her.

"There's no point in keeping it quiet, Becky. It will be everywhere tomorrow."

Zeeman looked concerned. "Bad news, Rhys?"

"You could say that. The police have been to see me. It seems our father didn't die of exposure. He was murdered."

CHAPTER TWELVE

There was silence, except for Axel Dorca exclaiming "No!" in a tone close to delight.

Helena glanced at him in disgust. "This is hardly a time for cheap gossip, Axel. If I hear that one word about our gathering here gets out, I'll know exactly who's to blame."

He reddened slightly, and pushed out his lower lip. I was left marveling that this adolescent in a man's body — albeit a tiny one — was an incredibly successful Internet entrepreneur.

Helena switched her attention to Rhys. "I'd appreciate the details."

Rhys was admirably succinct. The scattered bones of the male skeleton included the skull, and forensic examination had revealed that the subject had been shot once in the head. A rifle had been in the equipment for the trek, but this hadn't been found in the area. Dental records matched with the remaining teeth, and although a final identification depended on DNA analysis of bone samples, there was little doubt that these were the mortal remains of Oliver Hiddwing, founder of the Hiddwing Institute.

Will had his head down, so I couldn't see his expression, but Axel had recovered from Helena's rebuke and was bright eyed with curiosity. "So where's Clara? She was supposed to be with him, wasn't she?"

Rhys shut his eyes, pinching the bridge of his nose. "There's no trace yet."

Helena, ignoring the fact that some of us were still eating, fitted a cigarette into her ebony holder. "Unfortunate that Clara wasn't found at the same time, but I imagine dingoes and the like have dragged her bones all over the place the same way they did Oliver's."

Her lips formed a moue of distaste. "Perhaps *she* died of thirst." There was a pause while everyone contemplated this, then Helena added — showing, I thought, very little sympathy for the feelings of the bereaved — "Absolutely ghastly way to go."

In contrast to Helena, Gustave Zeeman was all sympathy. "This must be dreadful for you," he said, his face set in lines of deep commiseration. "I can only imagine how you must be feeling."

If he'd been closer to them, I was sure he would have clapped Rhys on the shoulder and patted Becky's hand.

Will said morosely, "It'll be nothing compared to how we'll feel when everyone knows about it. Jesus . . . *murder.*" He looked around as though someone might challenge the term. "That's what we're talking about here," he said. "Murder."

For the first time, Becky seemed strained. "This is a nightmare," she said.

A puff of smoke drifted over the table toward me. "Totally ludicrous at their age going out into such an inhospitable area," Helena declared. "I've never understood it, and I never will. I recall pointing out to Oliver several times how foolhardy these ridiculous wilderness hikes were at his age, but, as always, he pooh-poohed my concerns."

"They were both very experienced bushwalkers," said Rhys, his voice weary. "And they were extremely fit." He glanced around the table. "Fitter than anyone here, I'd say."

Axel cleared his throat. "I have a scenario," he said. He checked everyone out as though wanting approval, then went on, "How about this: They're both crazed with thirst, but Oliver, being the bigger of the two, is the worse off. Finally, desperate, he begs his sister to kill him. She puts him out of his misery, then wanders away to die herself."

Rhys Hiddwing's chair scraped as he stood up. "Father was found next to a permanent water hole," he said.

* * * * *

Coffee was served in a sitting room full of over-stuffed brocade furniture and murky oil paintings, most of which seemed to be of European landscapes.

"Part of Oliver's collection," said Helena, noticing me inspecting the paintings. "He had no taste in art, either." She made a wide gesture with her cigarette holder. "Oliver and Clara were in the throes of planning this building when they disappeared. For reasons that I cannot begin to imagine, Becky went ahead and followed their designs, up to and including the furnishings."

Raising her voice, she called to Becky, who was supervising the pouring of coffee, "This place is like a museum devoted to the late Victorian age, Becky. It would do a world of good to smarten it up with something modern, don't you think?"

I reflected that zillions of dollars and scads of undue political influence certainly gave Helena Court-Howerd the freedom to speak her very decided mind without fear of being slapped down by an irate recipient of her advice.

Becky came over to hand Helena a cup of coffee. "It's how my father wanted it," she said shortly.

When Helena's attention was caught by something inflammatory that Axel was saying, I took my coffee and made my way over to the cheese and crackers set out on the sideboard, which was in character with the rest of the room, being quite hideous. Nearby, Gustave Zeeman and Rhys were in low-voiced conversation. From their expressions, they were discussing something important, so I edged closer to them whilst ostensibly helping myself to what turned out to be superior blue vein cheese.

I've always had excellent hearing, and fortunately there was a lull in the other conversations in the room, so I heard Zeeman say urgently, his usual hail-fellow-well-met manner entirely absent, "It's your decision, Rhys. Do we put it on hold?"

Rhys was emphatic. "No, definitely not. Everything's in place."

"We'll only get one chance."

"You think I don't know that? We go ahead exactly as planned."

Zeeman ducked his head. "Good. I'm ready."

They broke off as the woman I would always think of as Mrs. Danvers approached with a platter of fruit and nuts. The conversation was apparently over, as Rhys, his face gray, made his apologies and left the room.

It seemed the evening was drawing to a premature close. Only Axel was still bouncing around on the balls of his feet, throwing comments and questions in all directions. After some effort, he managed to get Will, Gustave Zeeman, and Helena Court-Howerd into an argument about preservation of the remaining stands of Queensland's virgin rain forest.

I was drinking my second cup of coffee and half listening to their debate, which had Axel and Will pro the rain forest and Helena and Zeeman anti, when Becky called me over. She had collapsed into one of the fat chairs, and she gestured for me to sit in its bulging twin.

Obediently perching on the front of the chair — I had doubts I could extricate myself if I relaxed into its depths — I waited to see what she wanted.

She gave me a faint smile, then dropped her head, seemingly exhausted. "This situation is going to make the PR we did after the assassination attempt seem like a picnic. I imagine you have a very good idea how this murder story will play in the media."

"It depends on other news," I said. "If there are several big stories breaking at the same time, it'll be overshadowed."

"We can hope."

"If we're lucky," I said, "some Hollywood star will be caught making love to a duck." I grinned at her. "Or, better still, two ducks. Then it would be a ménage à trois."

Becky laughed. "You're a tonic, Denise. Come up to my apartment and have a nightcap."

"Will's giving me a lift home."

"He can wait." She got to her feet. "Come on."

We went up the main staircase. All the way up the first flight Oliver and Clara stared down at us. The portraits were similar to the ones at the Institute, but on a much larger scale. I looked at their painted faces and wondered what agony they had gone through before they died.

"Rhys has half the top floor, and I have the other," said Becky. "When Will stays here, he's in one of the cottages." She gave me a smile that implied, unless I was imagining it, an invitation. "You could stay the night. It'd be no trouble."

"I have to pack. I'm moving into a room in Jeffrey Karl's house tomorrow."

We reached the top floor. Becky flung open a door and waved me in. "My apartment. What do you think?"

Although it had nothing of the turgid bad taste of the rest of the house, I couldn't imagine ever fully relaxing in this place. The angular furniture looked to me as though it had been bolted together from a series of black-and-white rectangles, the lights set into the alternating black-and-white paneled walls were unadorned square glass boxes, and the mats on the shiny black floor all had the same pattern of geometric figures.

"It's very dramatic," I said, deciding this was not the time for brutal honesty.

Becky was pleased with my remark. "Exactly the effect I instructed my designer to achieve. And he has done that, I think, with the use of black and white, and the occasional accent of red."

The only curved lines I could see were in a truly revolting acrylic painting taking up most of one wall. It was composed of two gigantic red lips, slightly parted, with a drop that apparently was saliva spilling over the swollen bottom one.

Becky, seeing me regarding the painting, said, "You like the Bushconti? Cost a fortune, of course, but I love his work. This one's titled *I Could Eat You All Up*."

I made an indeterminate noise that could have been approval.

Becky gestured in the direction of the mirrored bar. "Champagne, perhaps?"

"Thank you, but I drink very little."

"Just to please me, do try a liqueur." She slipped behind the black bar to run her hand along a loaded glass shelf. "I can offer Kahlua, Galliano, Baileys, amaretto, Drambuie, Sambucca, or my favorite, crème de cacao. Surely something is to your taste?"

I hadn't had a liqueur for years, but remembered very well the jolt of alcohol the deceptively small glasses held. I wasn't driving, and thought I deserved a stiff drink, so I said, "Well, okay, I'll try crème de cacao."

"Join me at the bar."

We perched on thin-legged black bar stools, side by side, our elbows on the bar. Now that she was in her own surroundings, Becky seemed more at ease. She took a sip of her liqueur. "What would you think if you were a member of the public reading the story in a newspaper?"

I shrugged. "I'd be intrigued. I suppose I'd take it that they were ambushed and that your father was shot and his sister abducted." I considered for a moment, then went on, "Or something wild — like your Aunt Clara, for whatever reason, killed her brother and then disappeared."

"For seven years?"

I spread my palms. "I know it's farfetched."

Becky's manner suddenly changed. She leaned forward, looking at me thoughtfully. "Denise, I feel I can trust you. And to do your job properly, you need to know everything, so there'll be no surprises for you."

Not wanting to derail this unexpected sharing mood, I said gently, "What is there to know?"

Becky stared at her delicate liqueur glass, then threw back her head and emptied it. She grabbed the bottle and filled it up again, then gestured to my glass. "More?"

"No thanks." I took a ladylike sip. No way this woman was going to get me drunk.

She said in a confidential tone, "We've kept it quiet all these years, but when Oliver and Clara disappeared, so did a large chunk of the Institute's funds."

I was truly astonished. Nothing in ASIO's research had turned up this fact. "Someone at the Institute's an embezzler?"

"Not that we could find. The money was simply gone, and there was no way to find out how, or where it had ended up. Rhys and I had to use very creative accounting to cover up the loss."

"Could the person who took it have killed your father and aunt?"

"It's possible, but we just don't know."

She tossed back her second crème de cacao. I felt a qualm. This woman was well on the way to losing all her inhibitions, that is, if she had any to begin with.

Becky said, "We have a problem about this missing money. Of necessity, there are a few people who know about it, and now, with the pressure of what's happened, I'm almost sure there'll be a leak."

A platitude came automatically to my lips. "This must be a terrible worry for you."

She shook her head slowly. "You have no idea. Sometimes I feel I can hardly cope. Rhys is a wreck. It's like I'm the only one holding him together."

"Could Will help?"

"Will? Not likely." She poured yet another liqueur for herself, topped my glass up, then slid off her bar stool and paced around the room, the spike heels of her sandals clicking on the polished black floor. "Ilka should have been here tonight. She knows how to deal with Rhys."

"Where is she?" I inquired mildly.

"I have no idea. I asked Rhys and he snapped my head off."

Becky sat down beside me again, her knee touching mine.

It was time for a graceful departure. "It's getting late. I should go."

"No."

"No?"

She patted my knee. "Stay a little longer."

Here it comes.

The alcohol she'd consumed had blurred her smile. "You're very attractive, you know."

"Thank you."

"I hope it doesn't disturb you that I say that."

I went for bewilderment. "I'm not sure what you mean."

Becky laughed softly. "You know exactly what I mean. You caught my interest the first time I saw you. Do I have to spell it out?"

"I guess you're putting the hard word on me."

She frowned. "That's a harsh way of putting it."

"May I ask you a question?"

"Of course. Anything."

"Do I keep my job if I say no?"

Amused, she said sardonically, "But that would be sexual harassment, Denise. Surely you don't think I'd ever be guilty of that."

Raising an elegantly arched eyebrow, she went on, "Am I to understand you're turning me down?"

"I'm afraid so."

She looked me over. Her face was flushed, and I could almost imagine I could feel the heat radiating off her skin. She said in a husky voice, "I have a feeling you're not inexperienced..."

To my chagrin, I actually felt myself blush. "I really would like to go now."

I was relieved — and, if I were honest, just a little disappointed — when she led the way to the front door of her apartment. She took my hand. "But if you succumb to gentle persuasion in the future, I want to go on record as saying I'd be delighted."

"I'd prefer ecstatic," I murmured, unable, as always, to resist the smart line.

She gave me a long, speculative look. "You're more interesting than I thought," she said. "I look forward to knowing you much better."

CHAPTER THIRTEEN

The next morning I arrived with my meager possessions at Jeffrey's house. It wasn't early — I figured everyone deserved to sleep in a little on a Sunday. The drive over had reminded me of why I liked Brisbane so much. It had a clean, buoyant atmosphere, as though anything were possible and life was easy. This was rarely true, of course, but the optimism that filled the city was uplifting.

I parked behind the beige Volvo, which I noted had both a steering lock on the wheel and a window sticker declaring that the vehicle was fitted with an alarm. I was wondering if perhaps Jeffrey had chained a front wheel to the nearest lamppost when the man himself, his narrow face split by a grin, padded down the front steps to help me.

He seized my two suitcases as though they weighed nothing and started back up the stairs. "Terrific," he said with his usual heartwarming pleasure in seeing me. "I've been watching out for you."

It really was quite fascinating to be behind him when he was wearing shorts and a skin-tight top and see the action of the muscles in his overdeveloped physique. I had to remind myself that a normal-size skeleton supported all this brawn.

"Ah, jeez," said Jeffrey when we got to my new room, "I've forgotten to move the cartons with Vonny's things." He dropped my two suitcases and hurried over to pick up one of the cartons. "It'll only take a sec."

On an impulse, I seized the little pile of envelopes sitting on top of the carton. "I'll write *return to sender* and mail these back, if you like."

"Okay, thanks." He paused at the doorway. "We don't lock our bedrooms around here, but if you want, I'll put a lock on for you."

The last thing I wanted was to seem to have something to hide. "As long as the front and back doors are secure — oh, and the windows — that's all I need."

As I intended, this pleased him. "You're so right," he said. "The first line of defense against intruders is to make it difficult for them to get in. Now, if that line of defense fails and you have an intruder in the house, there are several things you must do immediately."

"Scream," I suggested.

Jeffrey gave me an oh-please look. "That seems to be your solution to everything, Denise."

"Works for me."

He frowned. "I doubt that very much. You obviously need to do a basic self-defense course. Fortunately the gym I belong to has exactly the right one for you running now. How about coming with me early tomorrow morning?"

"How early?" I asked doubtfully.

"The sparrows will have barely opened their beady little eyes," he said with a laugh.

I made a face at him, thinking that now I was really starting to like Jeffrey, even though I knew that at the very least he was a racist, and, for all I knew, possibly something much worse.

"You have to get fit for the wilderness retreat," he reminded me.

"I hear it's going to be in the Outback, not the rain forest."

"Who told you that?"

"Will Hiddwing."

Jeffrey wasn't happy. "It'll be bloody hot."

For someone of Jeffrey's build, the conditions would be even more onerous. "You could try and get out of it."

This hurt his pride. "I'm not the sort to give up because it's challenging."

"Me neither." I grinned at him. "Slogging through all that red sand with vultures circling overhead."

"Australia doesn't have vultures."

I waved an airy hand. "Well, you know what I mean."

When he left me to unpack, I went through the

missing Vonny's mail. There were the usual bills and a bank statement. The only personal item was an envelope with no return address that seemed to contain a greeting card.

With no compunction about Vonny Quigley's right to privacy, let alone the fact that I was technically breaking the law, I opened it. It was a card. On the front was a generic flower drooping with *Wish You Were Here* coming from its petal mouth. Inside was a terse message printed in block letters: VONNY, MAKE CONTACT. URGENT. There was no signature.

After unpacking I changed into running gear and went out to the kitchen to top up with water before I started out. Sam, still unshaven, was making tea, and Jeffrey was sitting at the table with the Sunday papers spread out before him. I'd already been through them at the hotel and knew there was no mention of foul play in Oliver Hiddwing's death. I'd also checked radio and television, with similar results. The story, for the moment, had died.

"You jog?" Jeffrey said, surprised.

I took a sip of water. "Only when someone's watching. Otherwise I walk quite fast."

It didn't worry me that he would offer to join me on a run because it was clear from his walking style that his huge thighs would make running more than awkward. As for Sam, he didn't look as if he could raise more than a half-hearted trot, at best.

Because it would be odd if I didn't ask, I nodded at the papers Jeffrey was reading. "Anything about the Hiddwings?"

"Not a thing, although I thought there might be, because there was a cop at the Institute on Friday. I get a feeling something's up."

"Such as what?"

He raised his thick shoulders. "Beats me, but Rhys sure looked sick afterward, when he was leaving for the day."

Sam, yawning widely, pulled out a chair and sat down. "Hey, Denise," he said. "We've got a booster brigade planned for Wednesday. I know you haven't had any training, but would you like to come along and see a little action?"

Apart from the fact that a booster brigade would be the last thing I'd want to join, there was no way I could be involved in disrupting a public meeting, as it was just the kind of activity that attracted television cameras. "Sorry," I said, with as much regret as I could muster. "I'm busy that night."

"Too bad. I'm setting up another booster for Saturday." With a sly smile, he added, "Jeffrey's coming, so maybe you're free then."

Jeffrey flushed.

"What have you been saying?" I asked him.

"Nothing."

Sam smirked.

"Jeffrey and I are just friends," I said with dignity. "And I wish I could come, but I'm busy on Saturday, too."

"That's a shame," said Sam. "You're missing a chance to bore it up the fucking greenies."

Before I left the house I went back to my room and grabbed Vonny Quigley's letters, putting them into a larger stamped envelope and sealing it, then folded it until I could cram it into my pocket. I trotted down the front steps, did a few desultory stretches, and set out at a slow lope in the direction that an earlier quick reconnaissance in my car had shown would lead me to the nearest shopping center.

As I ran I thought of how much someone like Jeffrey, situated at the front desk of an organization, could absorb. Receptionists knew everyone's comings and goings, they vetted visitors, and because they were in some sense invisible, they often overheard conversations and comments that weren't intended for general consumption.

I located a post office, checked to see that no one was watching, and quickly addressed the envelope to the ASIO covert box number, and pushed it through a mailing slot. Conveniently, although the post office was, of course, closed, there were phones situated in the shelter of its little foyer. A few people strolled by and there was light traffic on the road, but basically it was a sleepy Sunday morning and I had the bank of telephones to myself.

Myra sounded tired. "Did I get you up?" I said.

She yawned. "You did, actually. Very late night."

"I had one too, at the estate. A dinner party with some interesting guests, including Gustave Zeeman."

As best as my memory could recreate, I repeated the overheard conversation between Rhys and Zeeman.

"We haven't got any indications of anything significant in the works," said Myra. "This could be important. Find out what you can."

When I told her about the missing, apparently embezzled, money she was even more intrigued. "I'll find out who the Institute's accountants were at the time. There should be someone we can lean on for information."

After I explained about the envelope I'd just mailed to her, Myra said, "One interesting thing has come up about Vonny Quigley. She had an association with Australia's Redemption when she was at university."

"What sort of association?"

"She had an affair with Professor Sideworth, the academic who started the whole thing. The Hiddwings never would have hired her if they'd known."

"Perhaps they found out."

"Another item for your to-do list," said Myra cheerfully. She added in a more serious tone, "We're having another look at Sideworth's death, just in case it wasn't an accident." She paused, then said, "I know you're careful, but be *very* careful, okay?"

"Ever vigilant," I said.

"Speaking of vigilant," Myra said, "how are you getting on with Becky Hiddwing?"

"Last night I barely escaped with my virtue intact."

Myra laughed, immoderately.

I continued my run, but this time I was serious about it, looking for hills to get my heart rate up. I slowed to a walk, panting, after one particularly punishing incline, suddenly realizing why I had set such a punishing pace. I was angry with myself for wanting to call Roanna again. I'd only spoken to her yesterday, and that had been, to say the least, unfulfilling, so why was I yearning to hear her voice again?

It was, I decided, all Becky Hiddwing's fault. Last

night my skin had prickled with desire, not really for Becky, attractive though she was, but for Roanna. Later, I had slept badly, waking to fading dream images of erotic, pulse-pounding encounters.

On the next corner I could see the beacon of a public telephone booth. It was to be resisted at all costs.

"Roanna, it's me again."

"Darling."

I melted. Knowing what I was doing was wrong, wrong, wrong, I said, "What are you doing next weekend?"

"Meeting you, I imagine."

Having second thoughts, I said, "I want that more than anything in the world, but —"

"Can you make it to the Gold Coast?"

"What?"

"I have a friend who has a unit overlooking the beach at Surfers Paradise. He isn't there, and I can use it anytime."

"Roanna, I —"

"You're not going to say no, are you?"

"No," I said.

CHAPTER FOURTEEN

The next morning Jeffrey had me tottering around, more or less awake, at some ungodly hour. "It's barely daylight!" I yelped, but he was inexorable.

"It's only three times a week. You can sleep in all those other days."

"If you think I'm doing this more than once . . ."

It was a token protest, as I had every intention of complying with the regimen. Although I was already fit, I not only had to maintain that conditioning, I had to improve it if I was to sail through the coming torture trek in the desert. I'd use the defense class to warm up, then I'd go onto the machines.

Jeffrey drove. When we reached the gym — a mega fitness center with an extensive car park already filled with vehicles — I sank down in the passenger seat, not wanting anyone to think I approved of being in a Volvo in broad daylight, even as a passenger.

"Why are you doing that, Denise?" Jeffrey demanded.

"Doing what?"

"Hiding."

"It's fear," I said, "of making a fool of myself."

He smiled at me indulgently. "The guy who runs the self-defense class is a mate of mine. I'll tell him to go easy on you."

"You're too good to me," I said.

It was a very up-market facility, all mirrors and concealed lights and shiny equipment, and it was crowded with the usual devotees to physical fitness, many dressed in skin-tight, brightly colored outfits, although there were a few purists who defiantly wore ancient tops and tattered shorts. I was a happy medium, with a crisp white T-shirt and fresh blue shorts.

Jeffrey introduced me to Bill, the self-defense in-structor, who was quite alarmingly hyped up, hopping from foot to foot as he said, "No worries, Jeff, old mate. I'll make sure Denise feels at home and that nothing too drastic happens to her."

Jeffrey gave me a bracing clap on the shoulder and went off to the weight room. Bill had me sign a disclaimer, in case I was injured in the class, then bounced his way in the direction of a couple of gray-haired women. "Phyllis? Marge? Here's a newie to take under your wing."

Escorted by my two guardians, I joined the class in stretching exercises. The proportion was about two-thirds female to one-third male, and the age range was wide — from early teens right through to senior citizens.

It was a basic class, and Bill was quite a competent instructor, although of course he couldn't really give twenty or so people individual attention. I had the egotistical thought that I could probably take on most of the class and win, but I continued to play my role as wide-eyed novice.

It was soon obvious that class members took things very seriously. In a demonstration exercise, mildly-spoken, gray-haired Marge beat the bejesus out of a fortunately well-padded aggressor. When we teamed up in twos, thanks to my inattention I had the humiliation of having Phyllis whomp me so hard that I ended up on the floor.

This put me in just the mood for Arthur, a sleek, good-looking guy with an arrogant mouth. I'd overheard him making crude and disparaging remarks about certain elderly ladies in the class.

"Let's have a demonstration of a complete amateur coping with a street attack. Arthur, you can be the attacker. Denise, up in front here. You can play the victim."

Arthur leered at me. "I won't need any padding,"

he said when Bill offered him a protective vest that would cover his chest and crotch area. "This little lady won't lay a finger on me."

This assertion caused several of the ladies to make sounds of displeasure.

Bill then took me through the basic moves of breaking a rear stranglehold while Arthur lounged nearby, murmuring comments to an equally unappetizing male friend.

Bill was showing me basic stuff: a quick snap of the head back into the attacker's face, a swing of the hips to one side, followed by a fast backward blow to the groin.

When the friend snickered at something Arthur had said, my vow to remain an apparent neophyte went out the door. "Bill, what if I hurt Arthur?"

Several people smiled, including Bill and Arthur. Bill said, "It's unlikely, but the gym carries full insurance, and everyone in the class has signed a disclaimer."

"Just asking," I said, getting ready to be choked.

"Gotcha," said Arthur, getting behind me and looping his arm hard around my neck. He sniggered in my ear, "How'd you like to go down on me?"

I confess I used unnecessary violence. My head connected with his nose with an audible crack, then I swung my arm back so that my fist connected with his unpadded testicles with a satisfying thump.

"Ah, you bitch!"

I turned lightly on my feet. Arthur wasn't taking my defensive actions lightly. Blood running from his nose, his face suffused with pain and rage, he grabbed for my throat.

"Hey!" yelled Bill. "That's enough."

My hand-to-hand instructor would have been proud of me. I was efficient, quite graceful, and definitely effective. I broke Arthur's hold with my elbow, and when he swung wildly at me I delivered a straight-arm chin jab that snapped his head back. He tried to lunge at me again, so I was forced to hit him across the throat with the side of my hand, but carefully, so he'd be incapacitated but not seriously hurt.

Arthur fell at my feet, hands at his throat, making choking noises while blood poured from his nose.

I didn't say anything.

"My God!" said Bill.

Jeffrey halted at the entrance to the parking area to double-check each way before venturing onto the road. "I hear you put on quite a performance in Bill's class," he said.

"I'm not quite sure what happened. I lost my temper."

He looked at me sideways. "Are you telling me you've never done anything like a self-defense class before?"

"I've read books, and I was brought up with an elder brother who used to push me around."

"Remind me never to try pushing you around."

"Look," I said, "it was sort of instinctive. I had no idea I'd hurt him so much."

A smile tugged at the corner of Jeffrey's mouth. "I gather several of the female members of the class applauded."

"Well, yes, that was embarrassing."

Jeffrey shook his head. "Full of surprises, aren't you?"

The surprise to me was that I'd allowed myself to be carried away in the heat of the moment and that I hadn't considered how stupid it was to show these unexpected abilities. "Jeffrey, would you do me a favor?"

He chortled. "As long as you don't hit me."

"Please don't mention this to anyone else. I'm rather ashamed."

"You shouldn't be." He sounded quite admiring. "It was classic self-defense."

That wasn't what I wanted to hear. "I couldn't do it again, and please don't tell anyone I did it the first time."

"Okay."

We drove along for a few minutes in companionable silence, then I said, "I'd like to keep going to the gym, but I don't think I'll try the self-defense class again."

"Perhaps that would be wise," said Jeffrey.

Charlotte, whom I never met before, had come home from her weekend with Sid after I'd gone to bed. She was bustling around the kitchen in a tightly belted scarlet dressing gown, her short yellow hair standing on end. She had an attractive-ugly face and a sensational figure. "God," she said, "I hate Mondays."

"Hi. I'm Denise."

She waved the frying pan she was holding at me. "You want bacon and eggs? I'm cooking."

"I'm more a porridge person."

Charlotte looked at me as though I were some alien specimen. "Really? You're not into health foods in general, are you?"

"Of course not."

"That's a relief. Vonny had the whole place full of grains and yogurt, and wheat germ and God knows what. Not to mention vitamin pills and herbal things . . ." She shuddered. "Yech!"

"I'm nothing like that."

"Good. I don't think I could stand another one."

Checking out the cupboards, I found no porridge, but plenty of different varieties of high-fiber cereal, most being the type that tastes like the cardboard container it's in. I located bread and started looking for the toaster.

"In the lower corner cupboard," said Charlotte, correctly guessing the subject of my search.

"What happened to Vonny, do you think?" I asked in a casual, making-conversation tone as I put the kettle on for tea.

"She just got the hell out. She sort of hinted someone was stalking her, but she's a little mouse, no one would bother."

"Stalking? Jeez!" I said, injecting considerable alarm into my voice.

A snort from Charlotte put me in my place. "Oh relax," she said. "Sid checked it out and there was absolutely nothing to it. If you ask me, Vonny wanted to leave the Institute and she took the easy way out, packing up and leaving without a word."

"Jeffrey said she called."

She made a vague gesture with the spatula. "Oh yeah, that's right."

I was about to add that Vonny Quigley hadn't packed up but had left most of her things behind, when Jeffrey, half-dressed, came rushing into the kitchen: "Turn on the radio," he said.

Charlotte pushed a button on the cracked little radio that sat on the windowsill above the sink. Tinny and distorted, the announcer's voice filled the kitchen ". . . strange desert mystery. No statement yet from the family." An ad for car insurance came on.

"You've missed most of it," said Jeffrey, turning down the volume. "They've been saying murder in several different ways."

At the stove Charlotte flipped an egg with practiced ease. The delicious smell of frying bacon filled the air. "What are you talking about, Jeffrey?"

"Oliver Hiddwing. They're saying he didn't die from thirst. He was shot."

She didn't seem impressed. "Have they found Clara yet?"

"Not a trace."

"Then I figure she did him in."

Jeffrey was scandalized. "Don't let Rhys or Becky hear you saying that."

Charlotte shoveled the bacon and eggs onto a plate. I eyed it, sorry that I hadn't weakened and agreed to cholesterol plus.

"Rhys knows all about it," Charlotte said. "He's had me researching old stuff for the memorial service he's been planning," she said. "I've turned up lots of interesting information, including the fact that Oliver and Clara Hiddwing were at each other's throats just before they set off on their Outback trip."

"I don't believe it." Jeffrey was plainly annoyed. "There's never been any mention of a fight before this."

This amused Charlotte. "Like you'd know, Jeffrey, stuck on the reception desk like you are."

She took a forkful of her breakfast and chewed it thoroughly. My mouth watered, so I started hunting for something to put on my toast.

"It was in a series of handwritten memos between the Hiddwing seniors," said Charlotte indistinctly. She swallowed, and added more clearly, "Stashed away in a file at the back of a cabinet. If there was anything else about the fight, it'd been destroyed."

"What were they fighting about?" I asked.

"The usual," said Charlotte. "Money. And the direction the Institute was taking. I didn't read everything, because Rhys took the memos to show to Becky — at least that's what he said."

Her implied doubt spurred me to say, "You don't think that's the real reason he took them?"

Charlotte sniffed. "I imagine he wanted to bury the whole thing under the carpet, and I can't say I blame him. If they're dead and gone, why bring up old problems?"

I could think of several reasons why the memos might be important, and a motive for murder was one of them.

"I see the shit's hit the fan," said Sam, entering the kitchen. He looked quite presentable shaved and in a suit and tie. He dumped the morning paper on the table. The front page headline inaccurately declared: HIDDWING MYSTERY DISAPPEARANCE SOLVED.

The subheading said: SKELETON TELLS OF PATRIARCH'S VIOLENT DEATH. There was a photograph of Oliver, taken in his prime.

Jeffrey scowled at the paper. "Denise, you'd better go to work straightaway. The phones will be ringing off the hook."

"Yes, master."

He grinned at me. "In my dreams. You want a lift? I'm coming now, too."

I shook my head. "You'll spoil me with your car," I said. "I'd better stick to my common little Ford."

I was worried about media besieging the Institute and recording the images of everyone who entered, so I called in before I left and found that Sid had closed the building to the public, and had patrols guarding the entrances.

My fears were realized when I approached the parking entrance. A bunch of photographers were clustered, cameras at the ready. I was preparing to hide my face with a handkerchief, miming a heavy cold, but fortunately Becky's Jag was behind me, and she attracted all the attention.

Inside people were running around like disturbed ants. Elise, looking as though she'd been hauled through a hedge backward, called by my office to say she'd put the statement about Oliver that I'd okayed on Saturday up on the Institute's Web site and that she was frantically working on changes to cover the new cause of death. "I'll just get this up," she said, "and the bastards will find Clara, and I'll have to start again. And the bloody e-mails!" She threw up her hands. "You've got it easy, Denise."

The phone on my desk rang for the hundredth time. "I got the bloody phones," I said, "so I wouldn't call it easy."

The morning grew more frantic. It was assassination attempt furor, but doubled a couple of times, and instead of soliciting interviews, I was fielding persistent inquiries and basically beating reporters off with a stick.

At lunchtime Ilka came to collect me and take me down to the executive suites. She was her usual icy self. "You're calm, Ilka," I said as we got into the lift. "Everyone else is running round like chooks with their heads cut off."

She looked pained. "I've never panicked. I never will."

"Gosh. I wish I could say the same."

I was surprised at the shrewd glance she gave me. "I don't believe that you're as superficial as you appear."

"Thank you for the compliment."

"It wasn't a compliment," she said. "It was an observation."

Not liking the way this conversation was going, I said, "I expected to see you on Saturday night, at the estate."

Her face went blank. "I was otherwise engaged."

The lift door opened and she stalked off, leaving

me to hurry after her. I waved to Jeffrey as I passed his desk. His ear clamped to a phone, he sent me a distracted salute back.

"You've moved in with Jeffrey?" said Ilka when I caught up with her.

"Yesterday. Into Vonny Quigley's old room. Did you know Vonny?"

We'd reached the security door. Ilka turned her head to regard me with narrowed pale eyes. "You ask too many questions," she said.

Ilka didn't lead the way to Rhys or Becky's office, as I expected, but took me through to a miniature television studio. Sam, in his position as head of training and communication, was there with Becky and Rhys, along with a camera operator and a technician sitting at the control panel behind a glass window.

Becky gave me a wan smile. "Denise, I'm glad you're here."

Rhys was looking better, but he couldn't keep still, fiddling with equipment, sitting down, then getting up, until Becky snapped at him. I noticed that Ilka maintained a frosty silence, and he didn't approach her.

The Hiddwing Institute was going to release a short videotaped statement from Becky and Rhys, and Sam and I were there to polish their performances. My job was to fine-tune the words, Sam's to work on their presentation to the camera. In truth, normally neither Rhys nor Becky needed guidance at all. They were expert in projecting their attractive public personas, but the present situation had clearly unsettled both of them.

After an hour we took a break for coffee and

sandwiches. I was starving, but made an effort to eat moderately. Sam had no such inhibitions and crammed his mouth with food. Ilka, who still hadn't spoken to Rhys, had only coffee.

While we ate, we watched the practice interviews on the monitors. Both Becky and Rhys were excellent, combining just the right degree of measured shock, puzzlement, and dignity to suit the occasion. They ended by expressing confidence that the police would bring whoever was guilty to justice.

"Terrific," said Sam. "You really didn't need Denise or me."

Becky, sitting beside me, leaned over to whisper, "I really need you, Denise. Tonight."

CHAPTER FIFTEEN

The rest of the day seemed to pass in minutes, not hours. At five I went down to the executive suites with the schedule of media appearances for the next day. The videotape of Rhys and Becky's response to the news of the apparent murder of their father had been distributed to all news outlets, and I'd had a flood of calls requesting further personal interviews.

I expected Ilka, but Becky came down the corridor to open the security door for me. She glanced at the appearance schedule that I handed her and made a face. "This many?"

"I've even had calls from overseas. You'll be going out on a satellite feed."

In spite of myself, I'd been rather impressed by the fact I was being contacted by American networks and the BBC. It also put in perspective for me how very influential the Hiddwing Institute was as a representative of extremist right-wing views.

Before I'd gone undercover on this assignment, and had been on the outside looking in, I'd felt strongly negative about the holders of such extreme views, but now that I knew them as people, I'd somehow started to lose sight of the fact that they believed in these often hateful ideas. For example, I was beginning to think of Jeffrey as a friend, as long as I didn't hear him express anything to do with the Hiddwing doctrines.

Becky walked with me toward her brother's office. She stopped well short of his doorway and said, "I'd like to have dinner with you tonight."

I don't know why I was surprised at this direct frontal approach, but I was. "Dinner with you?"

"With me. Is that so hard?"

I thought quickly. Dinner I could handle. "Where?"

Becky chuckled. "Could I lure you to my apartment?"

"I'd rather not."

"Okay, then, I know a nice little Italian restaurant. We can sit in a booth at the back, out of sight."

There was a risk that some photographer would be lurking, but hell, I was hungry, and besides, it was part of my job to milk Becky for information. I said, "Sounds great," in a polite, not overly enthusiastic, manner.

We made arrangements to meet, and I continued on to Rhys's office. It was an unwelcome jolt to find Sid sitting there. He'd broken his dress code by wearing a deep blue short-sleeved shirt with his black pants. His intimidating demeanor was, however, the same.

Without ceremony, he said, "I've been wondering if you've solved the mystery of where you and Rhys met."

His bald head was so shiny it looked polished. I wondered idly if he shaved it every day. "I wouldn't call it a mystery," I protested.

Sid's lips tightened. "I don't like loose ends."

I contemplated a smart answer, but instead said mildly, "Neither do I." I smiled at Rhys. "I've been thinking about it, and I believe I know where you saw me."

Sid leaned forward, his blue eyes intent. "And where would that be?"

Myra had matched Rhys Hiddwing's schedule of appearances with my whereabouts, looking for a time when I could have conceivably been in the audience when he was speaking. She'd discovered a perfect occasion, some weeks before I had applied to work at the Melbourne branch. Rhys had been booked to address an anti-immigration meeting in Adelaide, but just as he was approaching the podium there'd been a bomb scare and the building had been cleared. It took so long for the police to search the area that Rhys was forced to leave for another engagement without giving his speech.

I recounted my story in as offhand a way as possible. I'd been visiting Adelaide, I said, and seen public notices of a meeting on an immigration issue I'd always strongly supported — namely no entry into Australia for anyone not white — and had gone along to join the crowd.

Rhys bought it; Sid, I could see, still had reservations.

Myra had briefed me with the necessary details. I described how there'd been several speakers and that since I didn't know much about the Hiddwing Institute then, the name Rhys Hiddwing on the program hadn't really meant a lot to me at the time. It was only after Rhys had said he knew my face that I'd thought back and realized this must be where he'd seen me before.

"So you were in the audience," Sid said, with just a hint of doubt in his voice. "And Rhys noticed you."

"I suppose he must have. The speakers walked up to the podium near where I was sitting." I put on a puzzled expression. "Honestly, Sid, I can't think of anywhere else where we were in the same place at the same time."

"Right."

I said to Rhys, "Did you see the bomb-sniffing dogs?" To add a further touch of veracity, I added, "German shepherds — big guys."

Rhys and I chatted for a moment about the dogs and the wonderful job they did, until Sid became restive and changed the subject to a security matter about the shredding of documents — or rather, the fact that some staff were failing to shred sensitive matter.

I listened politely, still with two burning questions in my mind. Where *had* Rhys really seen me? And would he remember?

I didn't go home to change, so I met Becky at the restaurant still wearing the chaste cream shirt and blue skirt I'd worn to work. The place was generic down-market Italian, with red-and-white checked tablecloths, candles stuck in wine bottles and mood-setting music just a touch too loud. She was already seated in the booth, as promised, in a back corner of the establishment.

We ordered: Becky angel hair pasta with lobster, me a simple penne with mushrooms. Without consultation, Becky asked for a bottle of Italian red wine.

When our glasses were full and the waiter had disappeared, she lifted her wine in a salute to me. "I keep thinking of you."

I'd mentally rehearsed my responses — at least verbal ones — if Becky was truly set on seducing me. "Do you?" I said neutrally.

"You'd blush to know what I've been imagining."

My traitorous body gave a throb of desire. "I'm your employee," I said.

She gave me a brilliant smile. "What are you saying? That it's unwise to combine work with pleasure?"

"Something like that."

Becky drank half of her red wine in one gulp. A

woman, I feared, of voracious appetites. My body pulsed.

I tried reason. "Becky, I believe in all the Institute stands for, and I want to contribute the best I can."

She watched me, amusement in her eyes. "You can contribute to me. I assure you it won't be a waste of your time."

"Well, that's very direct, but it doesn't change things. I don't think I could do my job properly if we were . . . involved."

"So I should fire you?"

I sighed. "That isn't quite what I meant."

Becky took time to wind her pasta around her fork. She put it neatly in her mouth and chewed, watching me across the table with eyes that, in the candlelight, literally seemed to burn.

Yikes! This is edging out of control.

"You intrigue me," she said. She paused while the waiter filled her glass again. When we were alone, she asked, "You feel something, don't you?"

Oh yes, I definitely felt something. "Not really," I said.

Becky laughed. "Liar."

I held on to a vision of Roanna. With Roanna, didn't I have something deeper, more significant, more everything than this? But still, we'd never made a firm commitment to each other. In many ways, we were still strangers.

You're rationalizing.

My skin felt tight and hot. I sipped some wine.

Becky broke a bread stick in half. I avoided gazing at her hands. She said, "I don't believe there's anyone special in your life at the moment."

"Well . . ."

Becky had the advantage of Hiddwing research. "No one at all," she said. "So there's no harm, is there?"

Pillow talk, said a wicked voice in my head. *Go to bed with her and she'll let slip information you won't get any other way.*

I was at that exhilarating point where my next decision could lead to tumultuous pleasure. But where was my will power? I was being skillfully seduced, and putting up very little resistance. "I can't do it," I said.

Becky reached over the table and ran a forefinger down my cheek. "Oh, come on. Let go." She was flushed, and her breathing had quickened, as mine had.

She said softly, "I've booked a suite in a hotel. It's only five minutes away."

I finished my glass of wine. "Okay," I said.

We drove separately to the hotel. I took special care, because my hands had an alarming tremor. It was a nice hotel — I'd have expected nothing less. Nothing seemed quite real. We met in the foyer, and, unspeaking, went up to the suite. I had the odd feeling that I was on autopilot.

At the door of the suite she had trouble manipulating the electronic key. "My hands are shaking," she said. "That's what you do to me."

I had planned to be civilized about this, perhaps engage in a little light patter once we were inside, but the moment the door closed behind us we were in each other's arms. She was literally trembling. Her mouth was volcanic in its heat. "Hurry," she gasped, sliding her hands under my shirt. "I've been waiting for this for so long."

"You've only known me a week," I pointed out.

She gave a husky laugh. "That's why I find you irresistible," she said. "You say the most unexpected things." She nuzzled my neck. "Do you do unexpected things too?"

"I'm very conventional," I said. "I prefer women on top."

A shiver ran through me as the air conditioning hit my bare skin. I couldn't imagine why steam wasn't rising from my body. I felt her fingernails run down my back. "Wow," I said.

It seemed only right to give as good as I got. She moaned as I kissed her, writhed against me as my hand slid between her legs. The bed seemed a long distance away, but we made it in a laughing tangle of arms and legs. There we fought each other, not for control, but for the heights of uncomplicated carnal pleasure.

She was tireless, athletic, merciless, as she caressed, drove, tortured me until I knew I was going to explode into fragments of white hot magma.

"Show me," she panted, "what you can do."

"I'm just an amateur," I said, taking her nipple in my teeth.

She wanted it rough, and fast. She wanted me to subdue the passion that raged in her. She taught me gluttony. I taught her patience.

In the early morning I left her sleeping, drove through the almost silent streets, and crept back to the refuge of my own room.

CHAPTER SIXTEEN

Tuesday could only be an anticlimax. No one at the house asked me why I'd come home so late, which was fortunate, as I wasn't up to manufacturing a convincing story. After a cold shower to shock me awake, I mainlined on coffee to get my eyes open, made it to the Institute without dozing off in the car, managed not to drive over any members of the small, but loudly vocal crowd in front of the building, and blearily dived into the depths of the car park. In my office, I collapsed into my chair and grimly began plowing through the calls I had to return, trying not to yawn.

I felt as though I'd had a comprehensive workout and that if I checked, there'd be bruises. A kaleidoscope of vivid flashbacks of Becky's naked, rapacious body kept popping into my head.

The incident was, I persuaded myself, a mad impulse that, in the long run, would mean nothing. In the short run, because of Roanna, I felt guilty as hell. Technically I could claim that I hadn't actually been unfaithful, as there was no agreement, no undertaking between Roanna and me. In reality, I felt both satiated and miserable.

The logical, unemotional approach was best: Last night was merely an event in an undercover assignment. For a moment I was amused by visualizing Myra's expression when she read my final report. Actually, there wasn't really much I could say. Perhaps I could pass it off as a strategy used to gain the subject's confidence. Unfortunately I didn't have the consolation of knowing that I had gained any valuable information — we hadn't had any extended conversations during the encounter.

And that's what it was: an encounter. Becky and I had made no promises, nor mentioned future assignations. In the end there was nothing but satisfied bodies and, in my case, an unquiet heart.

I didn't see Becky until midday, when a general meeting was called. The prime minister was still clinging to life but had been in a coma since the shooting, and medical bulletins had become increasingly pessimistic. In light of this, a coordinated response to the news of his death would be necessary, so representatives from each division were to give brief reports. For my part, I'd scribbled down a few key points and hoped I could wing it when the time came.

Ten of us were spaced around a massive blond conference table. Set in front of each place was a wafer-thin screen for audiovisual presentations. Copious refreshments were provided — the Hiddwings never stinted on supplies for the troops.

Having finally overdosed on coffee during the morning, I sipped tea instead, and chewed moodily on a chocolate doughnut. Sid nodded to me, taking a seat directly opposite. Ilka, I noticed, sat several places away from Rhys, then stared stonily into the distance, ignoring anything around her.

Rhys called the meeting to order. He was back to his positive, assertive self, and he delivered a truly rousing pep talk about how the Hiddwing Institute had challenges ahead that must be faced and conquered. It was a shame, I thought, that he was wasting so much natural talent on the promotion of such odious ideas.

Becky came in late, murmuring an apology, and took the chair next to Rhys. She seemed subdued, but not the least fatigued. She didn't look in my direction, which suited me, as I'd decided to play it cool, as though nothing had happened between us.

Sid got up to deliver his report in his grating, fingernails-on-chalkboard voice. There'd already been a mini-demonstration outside the Institute this morning, he said, so when Paggi died, he expected considerably more trouble with protesters and the attendant media personnel.

Elise, colorful in a gypsy blouse and full skirt,

delivered her Internet report with many exclamations and asides, but her skillful use of the visual displays in front of each person ensured that it also was extremely informative. "And whoever invented e-mails should be fried in oil," she said in conclusion. "Thousands! That's how many we're getting a day."

Bernie Miller, responsible for all travel arrangements, was a nasal-voiced, weedy guy with a bulbous nose. "I trust you're adding to our database the details of every new person who sends a positive e-mail to the Institute," he said officiously to Elise. "We need to keep track of our supporters in the general population."

Elise glowered at him. "Stick to travel, Bernie," she said. "I'm adding *every* name to the database, particularly anyone who criticizes the Institute."

Ilka came to life to add in ringing tones, "It is necessary to know our enemies, so we can deal with them efficiently."

This sounded chilling to me, particularly as I had a fair idea that Ilka, given enough power, would be capable of almost anything.

It was my turn next. I gave a brief report on the PR situation, mentioned the evidence of overseas interest to a murmur of approval, and finished with a comment that the media releases were being prepared now, in case the prime minister died.

"Oh, he'll die," said someone, "even if I have to go in and personally pull the plug."

Brod Coward, head of research, delivered a report on the range of government bodies involved in the investigation of the Paggi shooting, including his comments on the part each separate entity was taking. He reviewed the role of the federal police, and then I was fascinated to hear him bring up ASIO. As he spoke I looked at him with new respect, as his information, at least about my agency, was excellent.

He ended with a warning. "I urge us to be particularly vigilant at this time. It's more than likely that ASIO and other national security organizations will use the present situation to justify attempts to penetrate the Institute. I shouldn't have to remind you that anyone can be an undercover agent."

"Denise," said Rhys, "would you care to comment?"

It was like being hit in the face by an unexpected splash of cold water. "I'm sorry . . . ?"

"Would you comment on the PR aspects of national security surveillance of the Institute."

I scooped up my scattered wits and rammed them into place. "It's an opportunity," I began, not quite sure where I was going, "to publicly attack the covert actions of these branches of Australia's government who routinely spy on citizens going about their lawful business."

That actually sounded quite good. I was encouraged to add, "I believe we should preempt any plans by the national security forces to penetrate our organization by making a concentrated media assault on such clearly wrongful practices."

ASIO wasn't going to thank me for that, but the suggestion should have the result of cementing my position as a true-blue Hiddwingite.

Several other people spoke, and then Rhys got to his feet. "Recent events have meant a change regarding the upcoming wilderness retreat. Originally this was scheduled in a rain forest area, but the discovery of our father's body has altered our plans.

Becky and I have decided that, in order to praise the lives and achievements of Oliver and Clara Hiddwing, the retreat will take place in the Outback, and be coordinated with a memorial service to honor their memories. Full details will be distributed to every member of staff, and at least one representative of each section will participate in the wilderness expedition prior to the service."

There was a murmur of comment. Bernie Miller's voice rose above the others. "The heat can kill out there, Rhys. Surely you'll be putting lives in danger."

"Weakling," snapped Ilka.

Bernie's pale face flushed. "I don't consider it weak to question the wisdom of putting people at risk."

"Every possible precaution will be taken," said Rhys, his tone making it clear the subject was closed. "Now, if there's nothing else . . ."

Becky caught up with me as I joined the crowd trooping out of the meeting. "Last night was all I hoped for, and more." I was spared the necessity of a reply, as she hurried away, leaving me staring after her.

I thought of next weekend with Roanna. In my mind, I'd persuaded myself that one slip was okay, but to weaken and succumb to Becky twice would not be acceptable. The situation clearly was going to be a challenge.

Wednesday morning, after a good night's sleep and an early aerobics class at the gym — keeping well clear of the self-defense people — I bounded into work with something close to enthusiasm. I was starting to enjoy this public relations stuff, particularly as representing the Hiddwing Institute gave me a certain amount of clout, which was gratifying.

Rhys came into my office midmorning and sat down opposite me. "The DNA results are in," he said without preamble. "It's Dad, no doubt about it."

It was hard to know what to say. Oliver Hiddwing's death had been presumed for many years. "I'm sorry," I said, for lack of anything else to fill the silence between us.

He echoed my thoughts. "My grieving was over long ago. I've understood that he was dead for years. But now that it's official, I want a memorial service out where he died that will pay just homage to his memory." He stopped, frowning. "And Aunt Clara's memory too, of course."

"We mustn't forget Aunt Clara." There was a touch of mockery in Becky's voice. She stood in the doorway regarding us both. I looked from one to the other. Red hair, strong faces, vital, attractive personalities. Pity about the politics, though.

Becky came into the room. "What are you two up to?"

There was an odd note in her voice. Surely she couldn't be thinking there was anything between Rhys and me.

Rhys seemed to have picked it up too. He said, frowning, "We're discussing the memorial service."

Becky threw up her hands. "God, Rhys, you're getting obsessive about this, you realize that?"

His face darkened. "This is important, and you have to admit that, Becky. It's what our father would have wanted. And you know the other reason."

"What other reason?" I said.

A looked passed between them. My interest went up a notch. "Oh, nothing," said Rhys, offhand.

Becky leaned on my desk. I could smell her light perfume. She smiled at me, and said, "My brother isn't trying to persuade you that we can stage a media event in the middle of the Outback in summer, is he?"

Diplomacy was in order. "Well, I have been saying that it will be difficult to talk anyone into going out there when the temperature could fry eggs."

Becky turned to him. "I agree with Denise. It doesn't matter what inducements you offer, no one will go to the Red Heart this time of year."

I said, "I was going to suggest that you might consider hiring a professional crew and beaming the service via satellite to media feeds, and overseas too, of course."

"Overseas?" said Rhys. To his sister he said, "That would be perfect timing."

"It'd cost a lot," I said.

"Money's not a problem," said Rhys. "My father's confirmed death will release millions of dollars to the Institute." He glanced at Becky again. "It's fitting, isn't it?"

She nodded. "As though it were fate."

The week passed in what was becoming the customary blur of activity. I e-mailed, telephoned, became best buddies with a range of media connections. It was fun and exhausting. I also managed to fend Becky off, which wasn't too hard, as she was now fully committed to the telecasting of the memorial service. There was some hidden agenda there, but I had yet to find out what it was.

It was a relief to get to Friday. I ducked out of drinks with the office staff and came home. The kitchen was the heart of the house, so after dinner Jeffrey and I were sitting at the kitchen table chatting about nothing in particular when Sid and Charlotte came in to join us. Even though Sid had abandoned his usual black clothes and instead wore a white T-shirt and blue jeans, I still repressed a tingle of atavistic alarm at his presence.

"Denise," he said, with unwelcome enthusiasm.

I tried to match his tone. "Sid."

Charlotte grinned. She had a face custom-made for sardonic amusement, with peaked eyebrows and a mobile, cynical mouth. "I didn't know you two cared for each other."

"Just friends," I said. I got ready to get up and go, but Sid put a hand on my shoulder. "Stay and talk with us," he said. "If we're going to be friends, we need to know a lot more about each other."

I looked into his hard face to see if he was cat-and-mousing me, but his gimlet eyes were as innocent as they could conceivably be.

"Have a beer with us and relax," said Charlotte, ripping open a jumbo packet of potato chips and dumping them in a wooden bowl.

Jeffrey refused a can of beer. "Not in my diet, and shouldn't be in yours," he said severely. He ostentatiously got himself a bottle of water.

We settled ourselves comfortably around the old wooden table. I noticed Sid put a proprietary hand on Charlotte's thigh. I repressed a shudder. As far as I was concerned, going to bed with Sid would be like hopping under the sheets with a large reptile. Naturally Charlotte didn't share my opinion. She smiled at Sid and in turn put her hand on his thigh. I looked away. I was getting all thighed-out.

Jeffrey took a swig of water and announced, "I've just been telling Denise how she has to prepare mentally for the retreat. She's been to the gym three times this week, which is good, but it's a bit late to get into peak condition."

"Like you are, Jeffrey," I said with a tinge of sarcasm.

"Like I am," he agreed.

Sid smiled his dangerous smile at me. "I've heard interesting things about your activities at the gym. Seems you flattened some pest in the self-defense class. That right?"

I glared at Jeffrey, who looked contrite. "Sorry. I accidentally let it slip to Charlotte."

Charlotte laughed. "Don't you believe him — he couldn't wait to tell me. I would have loved to have seen it. Jeffrey said you broke the guy's nose."

"Not likely," I said. "He was a bleeder, that's all, and it was a lucky blow. I sort of caught him off guard."

Sid was looking at me in an assessing manner, which made me distinctly nervous. "Lucky blow?" he said. "I get the impression there were several blows."

"All lucky." I grabbed a handful of chips and crammed them into my mouth. It wasn't elegant, but it precluded me saying anything more. While I chewed I frowned in Jeffrey's direction. If he'd kept quiet, as I'd asked him to, Sid's interest wouldn't have been aroused.

Jeffrey, keen to change the subject, said, "What's

with Ilka lately? I asked her something this morning, and she nearly tore my head off my shoulders."

Charlotte rolled her lip in an impressive sneer. "Ilka Britten's a bitch," she said. "It took Rhys long enough to find that out."

"Ilka's on the outer with Rhys?" This was obviously news to Sid. "How do you know?"

"Will Hiddwing told me. Seems Ilka's been throwing her weight around lately, and Rhys told her to back off. Will said there was quite a scene after Ilka gave too much unsolicited advice about how to handle the discovery of Oliver Hiddwing's remains."

I took a swallow of beer and asked, "Are they lovers — Ilka and Rhys?"

Charlotte shrugged. "That's the gossip. What do you think, Sid?"

He was definite. "They're lovers. Or *were* lovers." He grinned. "Hope she doesn't hold you responsible for the breakup, Denise."

I was full of righteous indignation. "Me?"

"Yes," said Sid, "since you'll be partners, you and Ilka."

"What do you mean?"

There was a touch of malice in the amusement that filled Sid's face. "Rhys went through it with me this afternoon to cover all the security angles. He's finalized his grand plan for the whole Outback memorial thing. Teams of two are going to be dropped by helicopter at various compass points three days' trek from the place the body was found."

"You're not going to catch me doing that," said Charlotte, aggrieved. "I draw a line at slogging across the desert."

"No worries, darl, you'll be with me. But

Denise —" Sid broke off to wink at me. "Denise is stuck with Ilka."

I could imagine the pace Ilka would set, and I had a vision of myself desperately trying to keep up. "You're kidding me," I said hopefully.

"No kid," he said.

Jeffrey looked at me gloomily. "If I were your partner, I'd help you. Ilka's likely to leave you crawling in the dust."

CHAPTER SEVENTEEN

I had a clandestine meeting with Colin on Saturday afternoon. He'd set it up in a growled aside on Friday as we'd passed each other in the staff lunchroom, where he had been fixing some problem with shelving. It was a risk, so it had to be important.

Our rendezvous was yet another entertainment complex, though this one was the other side of town. It seemed I was destined never to see more than a succession of trailers and then, if I was lucky, the first scenes of the main feature. I bought my ticket to the movie Colin had chosen — naturally an alpha-male item whose advertising promised car chases, relentless violence, and recreational sex with large-breasted females when the action flagged for a moment.

I waited until the trailers had begun, then joined in behind a couple and wandered into the theater. Seven rows down on the left was an empty seat on the aisle, next to a bulky figure who'd put his jumbo-size popcorn to mark it as out of bounds. "Excuse me," I hissed, picking up the popcorn. "Is this seat taken?"

I ate it watching the screen while Colin whispered to me. Vonny Quigley's body had been found by a couple bushwalking in heavy vegetation fifty kilometers north of Brisbane. Her decomposed remains, identified by dental records, had been discovered in a gully fifty meters off the nearest track, and the evidence suggested she'd walked there under her own power and then been killed with a shotgun. There were no suspects. The postcard I'd forwarded to ASIO had been traced to a member of Australia's Redemption who confirmed that Vonny Quigley had decided to run her own amateur undercover operation and join the Institute to find evidence to discredit them, preferably by finding evidence of financial or personal scandals that could discredit Rhys and Becky Hiddwing.

As Colin spoke a dark sadness filled me. A woman I'd never met, but in whose bed I slept, had experienced terror, and then a lonely, violent death.

I'd finished the popcorn and hardly tasted any of it. On the screen one guy was busily beating another into a pulp. Colin said, "The decision's been made to keep her unidentified for the moment." He shifted in his seat, then said, "One more thing, and it's not good news. A run of surveillance tapes has turned up where Kookaburra could have seen your face."

I listened with a sense of cold dread. Rhys Hiddwing had been one of the many members of the public who were turned away from closed sessions of a treason trial where I had testified. There was a chance that he had caught a glimpse of me somewhere near the courtroom, or outside the building, after I'd given evidence. Precautions were always taken, but a casual glance, an unwary guard not turning everyone away before they could look through an open door . . . any of those were a grim possibility.

"You staying?" said Colin.

"I'm staying."

He pushed past me and left. He hadn't been asking if I'd continue to watch the picture, of course. He'd been asking if I'd evaluated my position and wanted to be pulled out of the assignment. I thought of that lonely grave in the bush. No way was I going to let whoever did that get away with it. No way.

Sunday was the only day Roanna could get away from the resort and a day I could hopefully disappear from Brisbane without suspicion. Surfer's Paradise was an hour or so south of Brisbane, set on a coastline of beautiful beach after beautiful beach. Roanna would fly to the mainland from her island far north off the Queensland coast, then change from a tiny plane to a commercial jet to fly to Coolangatta Airport. There she'd catch a cab to the penthouse.

I mentioned vaguely to Jeffrey that I was meeting a friend who'd come up from Sydney and that wouldn't be home on Sunday night, then escaped before he could quiz me further. "Don't do anything I wouldn't do," he called out after me. Originality was not one of Jeffrey's strengths.

First I drove to the car rental company and swapped my little Ford for a larger but just as anonymous model. Everyone was familiar with my car now, and I didn't want to make it easy for someone to follow me, if indeed anyone was. I'd studied my map carefully and didn't stay on the highway south, but skipped off onto side roads on several occasions in an effort to shake any tail.

We'd timed it so that Roanna would be in the penthouse at least an hour before I would arrive, as I had, of course, no key, and didn't want to linger anywhere outside where I could be spotted. I found myself tense with anticipation, and not all of it good. Becky Hiddwing and what we had so athletically done together swam in my consciousness, a slippery impediment to the uncomplicated joy I should be feeling at the thought of being with Roanna again.

"Oh, to hell with it," I said. I was determined to enjoy these few hours snatched, quite irregularly, from my undercover assignment. In fact, if ASIO ever found out, I suspected that I'd be severely disciplined. The trick was to make sure that didn't happen.

The building where Roanna was waiting for me stood with its tall fellows like sentinels overlooking the yellow sand of the beach. I had the code to the underground parking, so I drove straight in, punched in the numbers, and parked in the appointed place. I'd packed lightly — literally just a toothbrush and change of underwear, so I only had a shoulder bag as luggage.

An unfamiliar trepidation filled me as I rode up in

the lift. This relationship was assuming an importance I hadn't expected, and I was torn two ways. On one hand, I really didn't need the complications Roanna would bring to my professional life. On the other, I was afraid that I would find she didn't mean enough to me — that it had been a true case of absence making the heart grow fonder, and that when I saw her after all this time, she'd just be an attractive woman and not that special person she had grown to be in my mind.

"Hello," Roanna said, opening the door.

I walked in and she closed it behind me. "Hello," I echoed, feeling suddenly shy.

I followed her into the apartment, noting absently that it was coolly luxurious. My focus was on Roanna. She fitted perfectly the images I'd held in my heart. She was still the same familiar person — tall and dark-haired, with challenging eyes, an arrogant tilt to her chin, the hint of shuttered rebellion. There were subtle changes, though. The set of her mouth was more resolute than defiant, and her former coltish movements seemed to be transforming into an easy grace.

"You've changed," she said.

"It's the hair. I had it streaked."

Roanna grinned at me. "It's not the hair. It's *you*" She opened her arms. "Shall we kiss?"

"Might as well."

Her lips parted under mine. The familiar swell of passion and longing for completion flooded through me. It was going to be all right.

We didn't hurry. We had a leisurely evening meal out on the balcony overlooking the gunmetal sea. Roanna sipped champagne, but I declined. I was exquisitely tuned to the music Roanna's body was playing, and I didn't want any of my senses blurred.

She asked no questions about my work; I didn't inquire about the resort. We were in a gorgeous cocoon of affection and trust, and all our responsibilities and cares were for the moment held at bay.

We showered together but didn't make love there. We simply enjoyed the sensuous feel of skin and water. My body was impatient, but I held it under a tight rein until we stood together, arms around each other's waists, watching the stars come out over the darkening ocean.

"I want you, totally," I said, realizing with a shock I meant it. "I'm talking body and soul, and everything in between."

"Then we shouldn't wait one moment more." She turned to me.

Ah, but her mouth was luscious, her breasts against me kindling a warm tide, sweet as honey, that swept me into a singing passion. "Love me," I said. "Please."

"In every way."

Together we rose, floated, exploded. "Hard to do," I gasped, "that simultaneous stuff."

Roanna laughed, a throaty sound that resonated in my heart. If I could only have her feel what I was feeling, as I reached toward the possibility of something more than I had ever experienced before. To quiet the hammering of my anxious heart, I said facetiously, "If I say I love you, don't take it too seriously, will you?"

Her eyes were dark with desire, her body slick with sweat. "I understand," she said, "I really do."

And for the moment, I was content to think she did.

Driving back to Brisbane in the early peak hour traffic, I was filled with bitter regret. I wanted to stay with Roanna, not just for a day and a night, but for much, much longer. My mind sheered away from setting a finite time that *much longer* might cover. Her company was a delight to me. I smiled when I thought of her last words to me. "No one," she'd said, her face serious, "has meant as much to me. Hold that in your heart, okay?"

To take my mind off our parting, I turned on the car radio to hear solemn music and then the announcement that Albert Paggi had just died. His deputy, Heath Abbottson, would be sworn in immediately as prime minister.

I'd always thought the Australian system encouraged even more political backstabbing than usual, as the leader of the party in power automatically assumed the role of prime minister of the country. This led to unseemly scrambles for the top role in each political party, no matter whether it was in government or functioning as the opposition.

It seemed to me that Gustave Zeeman had this fact very much in mind. Over the past week he'd been everywhere on the media, each appearance shouting,

"Look at me! I'm prime minister material." He'd made statements, opened functions, been photographed with children — his preference seemed to be for the handicapped or those in hospitals — and otherwise acted as though he was on a one-man crusade to persuade the electorate that he was the one.

There was no pending general election, as we were in the middle of the present government's term, but his actions made sense if Zeeman intended to wrest the leadership of the party from the weak grasp of Heath Abbottson.

I felt strongly that there might be some link between Zeeman's media campaign and whatever it had been that Becky and Rhys had been referring to in my office. It was something that might coincide with the memorial service, but my gentle probings — any other sort could be disastrous — had got me nowhere.

Ilka might have been a source of information, but she seemed sunk in the deepest depression, and I could only get monosyllables from her, a change from her normal soapbox speeches. The only person she seemed to be talking to at length was, extraordinarily, Will Hiddwing. Perhaps she thought that Will would intercede for her with Rhys, but I didn't like her chances, because as far as I could see, Rhys had never treated his son with much respect.

The full weight of my assignment hit me as I got close to Brisbane. It was possible that Vonny Quigley had been killed by a homicidal stranger she'd met, but I believed that the trigger on the shotgun had been pulled by someone who worked for the Hiddwings — probably a person Vonny knew. Sid was my best guess. I couldn't imagine Rhys or Becky dirtying their hands.

They'd have asked for the problem to be dealt with, and given it no further thought.

Reticent, determined Vonny, believing so much in a cause that she risked her life and lost it. I wondered whose was the last face she saw.

"I'll get you," I said, "whoever you are."

CHAPTER EIGHTEEN

The Hiddwing Institute's media response to the prime minister's death went smoothly. We released a statement with appropriate expressions of regret that violence had sullied the political process in our country. Becky and Rhys made several subdued, respectful appearances on television and radio. I organized a letter-writing campaign, seemingly from private citizens, decrying the way the national security forces were using the tragedy as an excuse to hound and spy on innocent people.

On Friday Albert Paggi was given a state funeral,

attended by a broad spectrum of VIPs, including leaders of many countries and a British royal. I watched the pomp and circumstance of death on television in my office. There was something so moving about the slow march of the funeral procession, the silent crowds, the drum beating slowly.

"Surely you're not crying over Paggi," said Will, sticking his sandy head through the door.

I sniffed and blew my nose. "It's funerals," I said, "they always get to me. When I was a kid I cried for a day after burying my canary."

Will settled himself on a chair. "I've never had pets," he said. He grinned at me. "Dealing with humans is hard enough."

The camera inside the cathedral focused on Heath Abbottson, newly sworn in as leader of the country, as he prepared to give the eulogy.

"What a wuss Abbottson is," said Will. "He won't have much time to enjoy being PM."

"Why do you say that?"

He gave an overelaborate shrug. "Just a feeling I've got."

It was a feeling I was getting too. All week there'd been an unprecedented stream of visitors to the executive suite — Gustave Zeeman, Helena Court-Howerd, and Axel Dorca were included among the crowd of right-leaning politicians, business leaders, and ultra-conservative traditionalists.

"Gustave Zeeman's keen to be prime minister," I said.

Will nodded. "And he'd be a fine one, but Abbottson's got the party votes tied up." His light voice rose as he went on. "There are too many fucking bleeding-hearts in the cabinet. For the good of the country, they've got to go."

His vehemence was a surprise. I'd never seen Will toe the Hiddwing line with so much passion before.

I smiled at him, saying lightheartedly, "What are you suggesting? A coup?"

A fleeting expression crossed his face. "Of course not," he said. But it was enough for me. Will knew, or at least believed, that a takeover of the government was a possibility.

He was looking at me closely, a faint flush on his cheeks. Knowing that he was wondering if he'd said too much, I chuckled artlessly. "Hell," I said, "nothing that interesting would ever happen here, would it? Cutting off their beer is the only way you'd ever get Aussies to revolt."

I continued to chat inconsequentially with Will, all the while thinking that I needed hard evidence, not just rumors. That morning I'd gone to the executive suite with contracts for Rhys to sign to cover the orchestra, pop star, and media personnel associated with the desert memorial service. Ilka, her face set, had let me in, then disappeared. Rhys had been deep in conference with Zeeman when I'd entered the office, and he'd immediately covered the papers they were poring over so I couldn't catch a glimpse of them. While Zeeman did his usual how-glad-I-am-to-see-you routine, Rhys folded up the documents and put them in his wall safe.

I'd seen him use the safe before, and thought at the time how slack people could be, just because they believed they were protected by the security protocol of the building. The safe was opened with a key that

Rhys, like so many people, kept in a drawer of his desk. Even if he hadn't made this basic security mistake, the safe itself was an ineffective device that could be opened easily with a small charge of plastic explosive.

For really sensitive information I knew that Rhys would stick to old-fashioned ink and paper, and that he wouldn't carry it with him, as he was paranoid about being arrested and searched on the strength of some trumped-up charge. He certainly wouldn't put anything incriminating on his computer. We'd had a conversation earlier about hacking and computer security, and he had complained — quite accurately, since I knew ASIO had hacked into his system — that even sophisticated encryption programs didn't give total protection.

Will was saying something about the Outback trek. ". . . in the rescue vehicle."

A special events organizer had been brought in to coordinate the ceremony and telecast, and I'd been too busy with the PR for Paggi's funeral to pay much attention to the details. "Rescue vehicle?"

He grinned at me. "Surely you didn't think we'd leave you out there without backup?"

"I was hoping I didn't have to do it at all." I looked at him with suspicion. "So how come you're not part of a twosome striding across the desert plains?"

"I pulled family strings," he said. "I'm driving the rescue truck, which is air-conditioned, of course. And we've got a helicopter on standby in case something really serious happens."

"Have you been in that area before?"

"Not specifically there, but places like it. When you get down to it, everywhere in the Outback looks pretty much the same — dry red earth and rocks and that's about it."

"Super," I said, with no enthusiasm at all.

Very early Monday those staff members involved in what Rhys was now referring to grandly as The Homage Trek were to be flown in an executive jet to the site of the memorial ceremony, which was scheduled to take place at dawn on Thursday morning. Each two-person team was then to be taken by helicopter to separate sites, each three days' walk away. The teams were to set off to cover the distance in time to arrive for the service commemorating Oliver and Clara's lives.

Privately, I thought the whole concept was bordering on imbecilic, and several political cartoonists and commentators shared my view, but nothing was going to deter Rhys, who had the militant glow of a true believer whenever he spoke of the ceremony and its deeper meaning.

Becky was ambivalent. She liked the idea of honoring her father and aunt, but she saw, as Rhys did not, that there was a potential for mockery in the whole grandiose scheme. "I wanted to wait at least until Aunt Clara was found," she said to me on Friday afternoon.

"It may never happen."

Becky's voice was sharp. "Why? Do you think she's still alive?"

197

"I don't. I think her bones have been scattered by wild animals, and that if what's left is discovered, it'll be by sheer chance."

It was a fascinating mystery. Clara could be living somewhere in the world using the money that had disappeared from the Institute. Still, seven years was a long time to remain in hiding, and Clara Hiddwing's devotion to the Hiddwing cause made it all the more unlikely that she would stay incommunicado indefinitely. Unless, of course, she had murdered her brother. I examined Becky's charming face. Perhaps Clara was in touch with someone in the family, and had been, for years.

Becky misinterpreted my interest. "Yes," she said, "it's been too long. Tonight?"

"Becky, I'm sorry . . ."

Biting her lip, she looked at me reflectively. "Normally I don't like someone playing hard to get, but with you, it's exciting."

I could see the color rising in her throat. "Next weekend?" I said. "After the Homage Trek?"

She gave me a slow smile. "Next weekend," she purred, "will be an excellent time to celebrate many things."

Early Sunday evening seemed to be as good a time as any to break into Rhys's safe. Rhys and Becky had already left for the Outback, which got them out of the way, and a large proportion of the staff was scheduled to follow the next morning, so presumably most were occupied in getting ready for the coming ordeal.

Colin, as Col of maintenance, had already gained access to the building on a bogus repair call and had disabled the camera over the executive suite entrance. He would be waiting for me outside to take the material I retrieved, or, if the worst happened, to give the alarm to ASIO that one of their agents had been apprehended.

My first hurdle was bad-tempered Ed in the parking entrance booth, but I'd charmed him to such effect that he waved me to one of the executive parking spots, so I didn't have to descend into the depths of the earth to park.

I thanked the gods that Kevin was the security guard on duty. "Hey, hey, hey," he said, obviously pleased to have a break in the boredom. "And what are you doing here, Denise?"

"Nice mustache," I remarked. Kev had been growing it for the last two weeks.

"Now you're making me suspicious," he said. "Here to rob the place, are you?"

I feigned annoyance. "It's this bloody Homage Trek," I said. "I've got to get some special document for it from Rhys's office."

He looked troubled. "Love, I don't have the code to get in, so you've made a trip for nothing. You want me to call Will Hiddwing? He's probably upstairs right now."

"Hell, no. Rhys gave the entry code to me." I grinned at Kev. "He'll probably change it the moment he gets back. You can't have the underlings getting into the executive suites, can you?"

He followed me over, chatting, as I made my way past Jeffrey's empty reception desk and down the corridor to the security entrance. I frowned at the keypad, then punched in the numbers, hoping that there hadn't been a last-minute change in the code.

The door obediently opened. "See you in a couple of minutes," I said. I was in.

As soon as I entered Rhys's office I put on gloves, like any well-mannered safebreaker, and searched for the key. It was under a folder in the bottom drawer, so the plastic explosive and wiring Colin had given me was a precaution I hadn't needed. I opened the wall safe, took out the contents, and spread them on the desktop. Names, places, times. I couldn't believe the names that were there — two influential judges, several military officers whose names I recognized, a slew of right-wing politicians. It was all spelled out: Gustave Zeeman would assume leadership of his party, and those in it likely to dissent to this clearly illegal act would be arrested by the military on trumped-up charges. Heath Abbottson would be forced to step down, and a bloodless parliamentary coup would be complete. Several media magnates were noted as sympathetic, and guaranteeing positive editorial comment.

This damning information was contained in only a few pages, so I copied them all on the copier in Will's office and returned the originals to the safe, the copies to an envelope, the key to the drawer, and then myself to the safety of the building's lobby.

"Find what you wanted?" Kev asked.

"Sure did."

I talked with him for a few moments more, laughing when he said he had a vision of me goose-stepping with Ilka over the desert — everyone seemed to know I was teamed with her — and left with the envelope held casually in one clammy hand.

A few words with Ed, and then I was free. My heartbeat slowed a little. I could see Colin's lights behind me. He followed my car for three blocks, turned after me into a quiet street, drew up beside me, and smoothly took the envelope and the plastic explosive as I passed them through his window.

I watched his taillights disappear. Now he could worry about the information he carried, and I was free to concentrate on the rigors that faced me tomorrow.

CHAPTER NINETEEN

The pitiless sun hit the red earth and bounced back into my sweating face. I squinted to catch a last glimpse of the helicopter that had dropped Ilka and me in the middle of a bleak plain, etched into harsh lines by brazen heat and implacable time. As the beat of the chopper's blades faded and its dragonfly shape disappeared into the heat haze on the horizon, a singing silence descended. I looked around. Here was a world unchanged for eons. For a moment I could imagine we stood at the dawn of human history, and that the cities of teeming millions lay far in the future.

Such fancies were not for Ilka. "Come," she barked. "We need shade until the evening. Then we walk." She consulted her compass, then pointed. "That way."

I settled my dark glasses more firmly on my nose. Even with their protection, the glare was daunting. "Lead on, MacDuff." Ilka looked at me suspiciously. "Shakespeare," I said.

Our backpacks were heavy — mainly because of the water we had to carry to survive. Our map did show a water hole on our route, but we couldn't rely on it — it could be poisoned by some creature dying in the water, or it could be dry.

We were supposed to be roughing it, in the Hiddwing tradition, so we had no way to call for assistance if something went wrong. All the teams would be checked by helicopter fly-by halfway through the second day, and only then, if anything was amiss, would help be sent. "This is really dumb, isn't it?" I said. "Doing this ridiculous trek thing."

Ilka's lips thinned. "To test oneself to the ultimate is neither dumb nor ridiculous."

The shade we found was minuscule, and the heat radiated off the rocks as though they had some internal source of power. There were a few poor excuses for trees, lots of low, dusty shrubs, and clumps of spinifex grass, some several meters in diameter.

Jeffrey, of course, had given me detailed advice on surviving in the Outback, and I knew he would have approved of our attire. Like me, Ilka wore a wide-brimmed hat, long sleeves, and loose pants, as it was essential to cover as much of one's skin as possible. Sunburn could lead to heatstroke — and death. We both had thick socks and heavy hiking boots. Ilka had added a walking staff to her equipment. Looking at it, I thought that it could be a lethal weapon.

In fact, the walking staff was the only weapon we had between us, unless Ilka was packing a concealed gun. We didn't need arms for protection, as Australia had no dangerous animals who would stalk a human. Here, in the desert, the largest predator was the dingo. These wild dogs posed a threat to small creatures, and in one famous case, a baby — but they were more a nuisance than a danger to healthy, full-grown humans.

Ilka didn't look so much the chilly blonde in this temperature, but she still looked cooler than I did. She settled herself against the narrow trunk of a little, twisted tree and shut her eyes. Seeing her day to day at the Institute, it had been easy to forget her past history, to let the four suspicious deaths that had occurred to people she knew fade into forgetfulness. Now, totally alone with her under a pale blue sky, with no one anywhere near, those uncomfortable facts came back with force.

I looked at her hands: short, sensible nails on large square fingers. Had Ilka marched Vonny Quigley into the bush and murdered her there?

I said, "Have you ever killed anyone?"

Ilka opened her eyes. "What are you saying?"

"I'm asking if you've ever killed anyone."

There was a long pause. Perhaps she'd leap up and start beating me around the head with her staff, although in this heat that sounded all too energetic.

At last she said, "Why are you asking this?"

"I don't know. I suppose I was thinking about Oliver Hiddwing being shot."

To my surprise the topic invigorated Ilka. She sat up, saying, "I believe Clara planned her brother's death."

"You didn't know her, did you?"

"I came to the Institute afterward," she conceded, "but I've picked up enough information to form a firm opinion. Clara and her brother were at each other's throats about the direction the Institute was taking. Then she suggested the trek in the Outback. Rhys told me his father didn't really want to go but that Clara shamed him into it."

"And then she murdered him? Just because they disagreed?"

Ilka frowned. "You haven't heard about the money? I thought Becky would have told you everything." There was quite a measure of scorn in her last words. When I didn't respond, she went on, "After they disappeared, a large amount of money could not be accounted for, and no one has ever found it. It's my belief that Clara is alive somewhere, living the good life with that money."

"A third person may have killed them both."

"Perhaps." Her expression indicated that she didn't hold me in high esteem as a theorist. There was another pause, then the words came spilling out. "I told Rhys that his aunt had killed his father, and therefore she shouldn't be honored in any commemorative service, but he wouldn't listen to me. Clara Hiddwing destroyed the man who exemplified everything that I believe in."

Oh, please, not a speech in this heat!

"I have noticed," I said carefully, "that you and Rhys don't seem quite as close as usual..."

She turned her head to stare at me. "Will said it was your fault."

"Will said that? I don't see why."

"I thought you were dangerous from the first." Ilka was thoughtful. "I believed that if you had enough rope, you'd hang yourself, but that didn't happen. You ingratiated yourself with Becky, and persuaded Rhys that you knew your job. Any criticism I made was ignored."

"Gosh," I said, "you haven't had a good two weeks, have you?"

She looked at me, her face blank. I had a moment's regret that I hadn't brought some sort of weapon — a subcompact Glock would be nice — but the problem of explaining why Denise Brandt, tiptop PR person, had a lethal weapon of any type in her possession had stopped me from even considering such a move.

My trainer was always telling me to improvise. There were no hand-size stones near us. That left Ilka's staff. In an emergency, I supposed I could snatch it from her.

Ilka had slumped back against her desiccated tree. "I bear you no ill will," she said, her hint of an accent more pronounced than usual. "You're ambitious. There's nothing wrong with that." She peered at her watch, a big complicated device with multiple dials. "Two hours before we can begin walking. I suggest you sleep."

She pulled her hat down over her face. Clearly, the conversation was over.

* * * * *

I heard the engine first. I got up and scanned the horizon. The scorching orange sun was setting, and its rays blinded me. Then I saw it, a vehicle, made little by distance, heading straight for us, a plume of dust billowing behind it.

"It's Will," said Ilka, who had got up to stand beside me.

"Will? What in the hell is he doing here?"

She didn't answer. It seemed quite impossible in the heat, but I felt a cold finger run down my spine. Whatever was going to happen, I had a premonition it was not going to be good.

Ilka took off her hat and waved it. The truck, dust covered, jolted its way toward us. Will killed the engine, and leaned out of the window. "Evening, ladies."

Ilka, ramrod straight, chin up, said, "You've spoken to Rhys?"

"Yes. He's agreed we're to deal with the problem."

"He knows I'm helping you?"

He gave an impatient sigh. "Yes, he knows, and he's grateful."

I had the sinking feeling that the problem Will was referring to was me. "What's going on?" I said.

Will slid a rifle over the sill of the truck's window. The dark circle of the barrel pointed directly at my stomach. "You haven't been altogether truthful, Denise."

In dizzying speed my mind clicked through my few options. Grab the rifle? No, I wasn't close enough to do anything effective before he fired. Use Ilka as a human shield? That wouldn't work. She'd moved away from me, and was now standing in the balanced on-guard position for physical combat. Run? That was a definite no-no. There wasn't any cover, and even if he was a poor shot, in the truck he could catch up with me in a moment.

I said, bewilderment to the fore, "I have absolutely no idea what you're talking about."

He made a face at me. "Nice try, but Dad finally got it, over the weekend, where he's seen you before. It was just bad luck for you that he was watching a TV program on crimes against the state. It jogged his memory."

I shook my head. "What in the hell is this about?"

"It's about you lying, Denise. Sid was on to you a couple of days ago. You told Jeffrey you had an elder brother, but your application said you were an only child."

My stomach clenched. Until that moment I hadn't realized I'd made that slip when I was trying to explain to Jeffrey how I'd learned the roughhouse tactics to deal with the guy in the defense class.

"Jeffrey's got it wrong. He made a mistake." I might as well not have spoken.

Ilka said, "It'll be dark soon. I need to start walking."

"Deal with the water first."

Ilka went over to our equipment, emptied the contents of my water bottle onto the ground, then opened my pack and poured out the additional water supply into the dust.

I swallowed, suddenly feeling very thirsty. "What are you doing?"

They both ignored me. "I'm off," said Ilka, and without even glancing at me, she shrugged on her pack, picked up her staff, and strode away into the rapidly darkening desert air.

CHAPTER TWENTY

Will motioned for me to back up, then got out of the truck carefully, his eyes never leaving me. "We're going to wait until the moon's up. I don't want to run the chance of puncturing a tire on a sharp rock." He leaned against the side of his vehicle. "Sit down with your legs straight out in front of you."

I complied, acknowledging to myself that Will might be more formidable than I had thought. The pose he had me in made it impossible to get to my feet quickly, and he was careful to keep a safe distance between us. As it grew darker, perhaps I'd have a chance to run, but then in an hour or so the moon would be up, shining brightly from a cloudless sky.

Furtively I scanned the ground around us, trying to memorize where everything was before the darkness swept all details away. I concentrated on mapping rocks and clumps of bushes in relation to the truck. There was a shallow gully that might do for inadequate cover if I managed to escape.

Night was falling quickly, and stars were springing to life. With no city illuminations to dim their brilliance, they glittered in such profusion that they made an arch of light.

I tensed, ready to move if Will's attention wandered for a moment. Running probably wasn't an option. If I could get him closer to me, it might be better to attack him and take my chances. I wasn't going to be left to the agonies of thirst. It was preferable, surely, to have it over quickly. My logical mind said this; my heart quailed. I didn't want to die.

Will opened the driver's door so that the light from the cabin spilled across my ankles. "Move, even a little, and I'll shoot you."

"This seems a bit of an overreaction," I said. "I mean, if I was a little careless with a couple of facts . . . so what?"

"It's true, you know," he said conversationally, "after the first murder, it does get easier."

"And was your first murder Oliver or Clara?"

"Not bad, Denise." His face was shadowed, but he sounded pleased with himself. "Since you're so creative, I'd be interested to hear your thoughts. What do you think happened with them?"

"I reckon you were on Clara's side. I'm guessing here, but I believe she'd decided some time before to break with her brother, and had secretly transferred a lot of money from the Institute accounts. Then she suggested the trek, and Oliver wouldn't refuse to do it because it would look weak. Clara had told you their route, maybe even exactly where they would be at a specific time. I think you turned up in a four-wheel drive."

The light from the truck showed him nodding approvingly. "Not bad, so far."

"Did she shoot Oliver, or you?"

"I shot him." He could have been discussing the weather. "Aunt Clara was furious with me, because her plan was that we would take my grandfather deeper into the desert where there wasn't a trace of water, leave him with no supplies, and let him die from exposure." He paused, then added, "Pretty well what I'm going to do with you."

In a tone as matter-of-fact as his, I said, "And what was the cover story to be?"

"Aunt Clara was to go on with the trek, turning up dehydrated and desperate, saying that she and her brother had got separated, and that she'd continued on to get help."

"By shooting him you'd certainly put the kibosh on that scenario."

Will chuckled. "I drove off with her raving at me that I was a dumb kid who'd blown everything. In the beginning, when she'd been sharing her plans, she'd treated me like an adult, telling me I was the new generation who had to carry the Hiddwing torch into the next century. But now I'd shown some initiative of my own, she went right off her head."

"You could hardly blame her," I said.

"I suppose. Anyway, as we drove along she started

trying to work out an alternative story that would work. After a while I saw an outcrop of rocks and stopped. I got her out of the truck — I didn't want blood in it — and I shot her."

He made a sweeping gesture with his free hand. "Everything looks the same out here, but those boulders over there could even be the place. It was bloody hot, I remember, and I damned near killed myself covering her body with sand and rocks."

"And the money?"

"The bitch." His light tenor voice was no longer pleasant. "I thought she'd told me everything I needed to get the money, but she lied." He sounded outraged at this betrayal. "All I know is that somewhere in a Cayman Island bank is a lot more than a million dollars, just sitting there, earning interest."

"You went along with your great-aunt's scheme, just to get a chance at the money." My contemptuous statement, stirred him to action.

"Fuck the money," he snarled, taking a step toward me. "I thought Aunt Clara was going to let me *do* something — *be* someone. But she was just like Dad, using me." Bitterness flooded his voice as he went on, "You must have noticed no one ever listens to me. I'm a glorified servant, always on the premises ready to help. But I know everything that's going on . . . And I've done things none of them would ever dare to do."

Injecting a note of muted admiration into my voice, I said, "And you've kept quiet all these years, and not told anyone else."

"I've laughed to myself, hearing the wild theories people came up with. A couple of times I nearly told Dad the truth, just to show him I really was a

213

Hiddwing. If he knew, he'd look at me differently, but of course I can never tell him. Oliver was his father, after all." He shifted position, but the rifle remained steady. "That's what trips people up — they have to boast. I never have."

"But you're telling me about it."

"That's because you're not going to be around to repeat it to anyone."

"Did you blurt out all these achievements of yours to Vonny Quigley?"

Silence. I heard faint cracking sounds as the rocks around us cooled. "You're good," he said. "Very good. But, no — I didn't tell Vonny anything. She thought she was on a first date, and we were taking a romantic midnight drive."

"With a shotgun."

He straightened from his relaxed pose and took a step toward me. The light from the cabin glanced off the rifle barrel. "I'd like to know exactly who you are. My father will be interested."

"You're going to break your rules, and confess my murder to him, are you?"

"I'm going to tell him a little problem was looked after, like it was with Vonny." Will's familiar voice sounded mild and unthreatening. "Dad won't ask any questions. He doesn't want to hear the gruesome details." He made an amused sound. "Actually, Dad's on a roll with this memorial thing. If you're lucky, you'll have a little commemorative service of your own."

Over to the left of the truck I sensed a movement. In the faint, diffused light I saw the dingo slip stealthily behind cover. Then another one joined it.

I deliberately turned my head sharply, looking in that direction.

"That's an old trick," said Will.

Holding the rifle steady, he looked in that direction out of the corner of his eye. There was a rustle in the bushes, a definite sound that wasn't the wind, or a bird stirring. Will tensed, realizing something was there.

I called out, "Ilka! You've come back!"

Will involuntarily turned his head to look.

It seemed to me I moved with agonizing slowness, hearing the grains of sand grating under my boots, but before he turned back to me I was up and running into the night.

He fired, the flash at the barrel's end shockingly bright in the blackness. It was hard to hit a moving target at the best of times, and the bullet whined harmlessly off a rock. "I'll drive away and leave you," he shouted. "You'll die anyway."

I didn't have time to crouch down, so I was counting on the flash from the barrel, plus the light from the cabin, ruining his night sight. I frantically tore off my boots, then scrabbled for handfuls of small rocks.

Careless of whatever sharp things I might tread on, I sprinted in a wide circle around the truck, throwing the rocks at intervals so that they landed on the opposite side.

Will was losing it. He'd backed up until he was touching the truck, the light spilling over his shoulders as he fired several times, shouting, "I'll get you, you bitch. I'll get you." It was stupid of him: His own voice masked my approach.

I didn't have time for finesse. He stood within the shelter of the open driver's door. I vaulted over the front of the vehicle and slammed into it with all my weight and strength.

Will shrieked as the heavy metal door rammed the point of his elbow. I pulled the door back, then slammed it again. He dropped the rifle.

"Ah, God," he said, sliding down to a sitting position, cradling his shattered arm.

I snatched up the rifle. *No mercy*, my trainer always said to me.

Will looked up at me, mouth open, his face streaked with tears. His pain was not just physical — he'd failed a Hiddwing test.

I showed no mercy. "It's a pity," I said, "but I don't believe your father will think well of you for this."

CHAPTER TWENTY-ONE

I drove the truck back to the central point where the memorial service was to have been held, Will groaning in the passenger seat. I'd tied him in, but it wasn't really necessary, as he was curled in on himself, his insouciant persona collapsed in pain and failure.

When I drove into the site, the federal police and the military were already there in force. Obviously the pages I'd copied and given to Colin had borne fruit, and the Hiddwings' scheme had be thwarted before it had any chance of being implemented.

Half-erected tiers of seating formed a semicircle around a central altar, and nearby was a huge white tent, which apparently had been appropriated as a processing center. Shell-shocked Hiddwing staff were standing in lines, waiting to be interviewed.

I turned Will over to the nearest officer, who immediately summoned a medical team to tend to him, and then I reported to the person in charge, a cool-faced woman with a high rank. There were several ASIO representatives present, and they used their considerable influence to make sure that I had the minimum of explaining to do. A military party was sent out to intercept, and arrest, Ilka Britten.

I felt the letdown of anticlimax. I hadn't slept for twenty-four hours, and my whole time in the desert seemed surreal. I arranged to have a seat on a chartered federal police flight back to Brisbane that was leaving in two hours. The heavy weight of the heat pressed down on my shoulders. It wasn't admirable, but I wanted to see the Hiddwings after they'd been humbled. I waited by a smaller tent that apparently had been intended as the Hiddwings' personal lodgings but was now the army's preserve.

Rhys came out first. He was handcuffed, but he wore the shackles as though they didn't exist. He stopped short when he saw me. One of the officers escorting him tugged at his arm, but Rhys didn't move. We shared a long, adversarial look, then he turned his face away and began walking toward the waiting military helicopter.

Becky was next. She was solemn, calm. She saw

me and, extraordinarily, a small smile tugged at her mouth. "You're quite a woman," she said.

I didn't reply, but I watched her until she disappeared into the helicopter and it lifted off in the pale, pale sky.

CHAPTER TWENTY-TWO

ATTEMPTED COUP FAILS screamed the headlines. RIGHT-WING CONSPIRACY THWARTED. HIDDWINGS LINKED TO PAGGI MURDER.

Talking heads on television pontificated. Talk radio swelled with anxious or rabid or confused voices. The roll of those arrested was large, and a number of careers were seriously dented, if not destroyed. Apart from Becky, Rhys, and Will Hiddwing, Ilka Britten and Gustave Zeeman had been arrested. Helena Court-

Howerd and Axel Dorca were under active investigation, as were a number of the judiciary and mid-ranking military officers.

I knew that many details would never be released, and in time it was likely that it would become in the public imagination just a tin-pot attempt to overthrow the government. The Hiddwing Institute was discredited, but many adherents were vowing to keep it alive for the time — in my estimation, when hell froze over — when Rhys and Becky would be freed.

Before I went back to Canberra I saw Jeffrey one more time, when I went back to collect my things from the room in his house. He looked at me strangely, as though he'd never seen me before. "Is your name really Denise?" he said.

"It's really Denise." I handed him an envelope. "My rent for the rest of the month."

"You're not planning to stay here!" Wriggling his heavy shoulders uncomfortably, he added, "What I mean is, now Sid's been arrested, I don't think Charlotte would be all that pleased to see you again."

"I'm not staying."

Jeffrey's expression combined relief and regret in about equal quantities. "I won't take your money, then."

"It's in lieu of notice for my sudden departure." On an impulse, I leaned over and kissed his cheek. "Jeffrey," I said, "don't let those Institute ideas hold you back from the world outside, will you?"

He stared at me, then said with the slightest of smiles, "I'll try not to."

* * * * *

I had been de-programmed, de-briefed, de-everythinged. I sat in my own dear kitchen and watched the birds clustering on the feeder hanging outside the door. I wished I had a cat — two cats, perhaps. And a dog, a wiggling, cheerful bitzer who'd treat me like a deity. Of course I couldn't have any pets at the moment, not when I was liable to be undercover for months at a time.

To be so close to death had made me stingingly aware of living. I wanted to call Roanna, tell her I was all right. "I'm alive," I'd say. "I could have been dead, but I'm alive!"

She'd be puzzled; she wouldn't know that I'd been under any threat. That I'd been in danger of leaving light and laughter behind forever.

Besides, ASIO would frown on such a contact. Frown? I would be forbidden to make the call.

I picked up the receiver, punched in her number.

"Roanna," I said. "I'm alive."

CLAIRE McNAB, author of the exciting
Denise Cleever thrillers and the famous
Detective Inspector Carol Ashton mysteries.

LOOKING FOR NAIAD?

Buy our books at
www.naiadpress.com

or call our toll-free number
1-800-533-1973

or by fax (24 hours a day)
1-850-539-9731

A few of the publications of
THE NAIAD PRESS, INC.
P.O. Box 10543   Tallahassee, Florida 32302
Phone (850) 539-5965
Toll-Free Order Number: 1-800-533-1973
Web Site: WWW.NAIADPRESS.COM
Mail orders welcome. Please include 15% postage.
Write or call for our free catalog which also features an
incredible selection of lesbian videos.

DEATH UNDERSTOOD by Claire McNab. 240 pp. 2nd Denise Cleever
thriller.   ISBN 1-56280-264-X $11.95

TREASURED PAST by Linda Hill. 208 pp. A shared passion for
antiques leads to love.   ISBN 1-56280-263-1 $11.95

UNDER SUSPICION by Claire McNab. 224 pp. 12th Detective
Inspector Carol Ashton mystery.   ISBN 1-56280-261-5 $11.95

UNFORGETTABLE by Karin Kallmaker. 288 pp. Can each
woman win her true love's heart?   ISBN 1-56280-260-7   11.95

MURDER UNDERCOVER by Claire McNab. 192 pp. 1st Denise
Cleever thriller.   ISBN 1-56280-259-3   11.95

EVERYTIME WE SAY GOODBYE by Jaye Maiman. 272 pp.
7th Robin Miller mystery.   ISBN 1-56280-248-8   11.95

SEVENTH HEAVEN by Kate Calloway. 240 pp. 7th Cassidy
James mystery.   ISBN 1-56280-262-3   11.95

STRANGERS IN THE NIGHT by Barbara Johnson. 208 pp. Her
body and soul react to a stranger's touch.   ISBN 1-56280-256-9   11.95

THE VERY THOUGHT OF YOU edited by Barbara Grier and
Christine Cassidy. 288 pp. Erotic love stories by Naiad Press
authors.   ISBN 1-56280-250-X   14.95

TO HAVE AND TO HOLD by PeGGy J. Herring. 192 pp. Their
friendship grows to intense passion . . .   ISBN 1-56280-251-8   11.95

INTIMATE STRANGER by Laura DeHart Young. 192 pp.
Ignoring Tray's myserious past, could Cole be playing with fire?
                                             ISBN 1-56280-249-6   11.95

SHATTERED ILLUSIONS by Kaye Davis. 256 pp. 4th
Maris Middleton mystery.   ISBN 1-56280-252-6   11.95

SET UP by Claire McNab. 224 pp. 11th Detective Inspector Carol
Ashton mystery.   ISBN 1-56280-255-0   11.95

THE DAWNING by Laura Adams. 224 pp. What if you had the
power to change the past? ISBN 1-56280-246-1 11.95

NEVER ENDING by Marianne K. Martin. 224 pp. Temptation
appears in the form of an old friend and lover. ISBN 1-56280-247-X 11.95

ONE OF OUR OWN by Diane Salvatore. 240 pp. Carly Matson
has a secret. So does Lela Johns. ISBN 1-56280-243-7 11.95

DOUBLE TAKEOUT by Tracey Richardson. 176 pp. 3rd Stevie
Houston mystery. ISBN 1-56280-244-5 11.95

CAPTIVE HEART by Frankie J. Jones. 176 pp. Love in the
fast lane or heartside romance? ISBN 1-56280-258-5 11.95

WICKED GOOD TIME by Diana Tremain Braund. 224 pp. In
charge at work, out of control in her heart. ISBN 1-56280-241-0 11.95

SNAKE EYES by Pat Welch. 256 pp. 7th Helen Black mystery.
ISBN 1-56280-242-9 11.95

CHANGE OF HEART by Linda Hill. 176 pp. High fashion and
love in a glamorous world. ISBN 1-56280-238-0 11.95

UNSTRUNG HEART by Robbi Sommers. 176 pp. Putting life
in order again. ISBN 1-56280-239-9 11.95

BIRDS OF A FEATHER by Jackie Calhoun. 240 pp. Life begins
with love. ISBN 1-56280-240-2 11.95

THE DRIVE by Trisha Todd. 176 pp. The star of *Claire of the
Moon* tells all! ISBN 1-56280-237-2 11.95

BOTH SIDES by Saxon Bennett. 240 pp. A community of
women falling in and out of love. ISBN 1-56280-236-4 11.95

WATERMARK by Karin Kallmaker. 256 pp. One burning
question . . . how to lead her back to love? ISBN 1-56280-235-6 11.95

THE OTHER WOMAN by Ann O'Leary. 240 pp. Her roguish
way draws women like a magnet. ISBN 1-56280-234-8 11.95

SILVER THREADS by Lyn Denison.208 pp. Finding her way
back to love . . . ISBN 1-56280-231-3 11.95

CHIMNEY ROCK BLUES by Janet McClellan. 224 pp. 4th Tru
North mystery. ISBN 1-56280-233-X 11.95

OMAHA'S BELL by Penny Hayes. 208 pp. Orphaned Keeley
Delaney woos the lovely Prudence Morris. ISBN 1-56280-232-1 11.95

SIXTH SENSE by Kate Calloway. 224 pp. 6th Cassidy James
mystery. ISBN 1-56280-228-3 11.95

DAWN OF THE DANCE by Marianne K. Martin. 224 pp. A dance
with an old friend, nothing more . . . yeah! ISBN 1-56280-229-1 11.95

THOSE WHO WAIT by Peggy J. Herring. 160 pp. Two
sisters . . . in love with the same woman. ISBN 1-56280-223-2 11.95

WHISPERS IN THE WIND by Frankie J. Jones. 192 pp. "If you don't want this," she whispered, "all you have to say is 'stop.'"
ISBN 1-56280-226-7   11.95

WHEN SOME BODY DISAPPEARS by Therese Szymanski. 192 pp. 3rd Brett Higgins mystery.   ISBN 1-56280-227-5   11.95

UNTIL THE END by Kaye Davis. 256pp. 3rd Maris Middleton mystery.   ISBN 1-56280-222-4   11.95

FIFTH WHEEL by Kate Calloway. 224 pp. 5th Cassidy James mystery.   ISBN 1-56280-218-6   11.95

JUST YESTERDAY by Linda Hill. 176 pp. Reliving all the passion of yesterday.   ISBN 1-56280-219-4   11.95

THE TOUCH OF YOUR HAND edited by Barbara Grier and Christine Cassidy. 304 pp. Erotic love stories by Naiad Press authors.   ISBN 1-56280-220-8   14.95

WINDROW GARDEN by Janet McClellan. 192 pp. They discover a passion they never dreamed possible.   ISBN 1-56280-216-X   11.95

PAST DUE by Claire McNab. 224 pp. 10th Carol Ashton mystery.   ISBN 1-56280-217-8   11.95

CHRISTABEL by Laura Adams. 224 pp. Two captive hearts and the passion that will set them free.   ISBN 1-56280-214-3   11.95

PRIVATE PASSIONS by Laura DeHart Young. 192 pp. An unforgettable new portrait of lesbian love . . .   ISBN 1-56280-215-1   11.95

BAD MOON RISING by Barbara Johnson. 208 pp. 2nd Colleen Fitzgerald mystery.   ISBN 1-56280-211-9   11.95

RIVER QUAY by Janet McClellan. 208 pp. 3rd Tru North mystery.   ISBN 1-56280-212-7   11.95

ENDLESS LOVE by Lisa Shapiro. 272 pp. To believe, once again, that love can be forever.   ISBN 1-56280-213-5   11.95

FALLEN FROM GRACE by Pat Welch. 256 pp. 6th Helen Black mystery.   ISBN 1-56280-209-7   11.95

THE NAKED EYE by Catherine Ennis. 208 pp. Her lover in the camera's eye . . .   ISBN 1-56280-210-0   11.95

OVER THE LINE by Tracey Richardson. 176 pp. 2nd Stevie Houston mystery.   ISBN 1-56280-202-X   11.95

LOVE IN THE BALANCE by Marianne K. Martin. 256 pp. Weighing the costs of love . . .   ISBN 1-56280-199-6   11.95

PIECE OF MY HEART by Julia Watts. 208 pp. All the stuff that dreams are made of —   ISBN 1-56280-206-2   11.95

MAKING UP FOR LOST TIME by Karin Kallmaker. 240 pp. Nobody does it better . . .   ISBN 1-56280-196-1   11.95

GOLD FEVER by Lyn Denison. 224 pp. By author of *Dream Lover*.   ISBN 1-56280-201-1   11.95

WHEN THE DEAD SPEAK by Therese Szymanski. 224 pp. 2nd
Brett Higgins mystery.   ISBN 1-56280-198-8   11.95
FOURTH DOWN by Kate Calloway. 240 pp. 4th Cassidy James
mystery.   ISBN 1-56280-193-7   11.95
CITY LIGHTS COUNTRY CANDLES by Penny Hayes. 208 pp.
About the women she has known . . .   ISBN 1-56280-195-3   11.95
POSSESSIONS by Kaye Davis. 240 pp. 2nd Maris Middleton
mystery.   ISBN 1-56280-192-9   11.95
A QUESTION OF LOVE by Saxon Bennett. 208 pp. Every
woman is granted one great love.   ISBN 1-56280-205-4   11.95
RHYTHM TIDE by Frankie J. Jones. 160 pp. . . . to desire
passionately and be passionately desired. ISBN 1-56280-189-9   11.95
PENN VALLEY PHOENIX by Janet McClellan. 208 pp. 2nd
Tru North Mystery.   ISBN 1-56280-200-3   11.95
OLD BLACK MAGIC by Jaye Maiman. 272 pp. 6th Robin
Miller mystery.   ISBN 1-56280-175-9   11.95
LEGACY OF LOVE by Marianne K. Martin. 240 pp. Women
will do anything for her . . .   ISBN 1-56280-184-8   11.95
LETTING GO by Ann O'Leary. 160 pp. Laura, at 39, in love
with 23-year-old Kate.   ISBN 1-56280-183-X   11.95
LADY BE GOOD edited by Barbara Grier and Christine Cassidy.
288 pp. Erotic stories by Naiad Press authors. ISBN 1-56280-180-5   14.95
CHAIN LETTER by Claire McNab. 288 pp. 9th Carol Ashton
mystery.   ISBN 1-56280-181-3   11.95
NIGHT VISION by Laura Adams. 256 pp. Erotic fantasy romance
by "famous" author.   ISBN 1-56280-182-1   11.95
SEA TO SHINING SEA by Lisa Shapiro. 256 pp. Unable to resist
the raging passion . . .   ISBN 1-56280-177-5   11.95
THIRD DEGREE by Kate Calloway. 224 pp. 3rd Cassidy James
mystery.   ISBN 1-56280-185-6   11.95
WHEN THE DANCING STOPS by Therese Szymanski. 272 pp.
1st Brett Higgins mystery.   ISBN 1-56280-186-4   11.95
PHASES OF THE MOON by Julia Watts. 192 pp. . . . . hungry
for everything life has to offer.   ISBN 1-56280-176-7   11.95
BABY IT'S COLD by Jaye Maiman. 256 pp. 5th Robin Miller
mystery.   ISBN 1-56280-156-2   10.95
CLASS REUNION by Linda Hill. 176 pp. The girl from her
past . . .   ISBN 1-56280-178-3   11.95
DREAM LOVER by Lyn Denison. 224 pp. A soft, sensuous,
romantic fantasy.   ISBN 1-56280-173-2   11.95
FORTY LOVE by Diana Simmonds. 288 pp. Joyous, heartwarming romance.   ISBN 1-56280-171-6   11.95

IN THE MOOD by Robbi Sommers. 160 pp. The queen of
erotic tension! ISBN 1-56280-172-4 11.95

SWIMMING CAT COVE by Lauren Wright Douglas. 192 pp. 2nd
Allison O'Neil Mystery. ISBN 1-56280-168-6 11.95

THE LOVING LESBIAN by Claire McNab and Sharon Gedan.
240 pp. Explore the experiences that make lesbian love unique.
ISBN 1-56280-169-4 14.95

COURTED by Celia Cohen. 160 pp. Sparkling romantic
encounter. ISBN 1-56280-166-X 11.95

SEASONS OF THE HEART by Jackie Calhoun. 240 pp. Romance
through the years. ISBN 1-56280-167-8 11.95

K. C. BOMBER by Janet McClellan. 208 pp. 1st Tru North
mystery. ISBN 1-56280-157-0 11.95

LAST RITES by Tracey Richardson. 192 pp. 1st Stevie Houston
mystery. ISBN 1-56280-164-3 11.95

EMBRACE IN MOTION by Karin Kallmaker. 256 pp. A whirlwind
love affair. ISBN 1-56280-165-1 11.95

HOT CHECK by Peggy J. Herring. 192 pp. Will workaholic Alice
fall for guitarist Ricky? ISBN 1-56280-163-5 11.95

OLD TIES by Saxon Bennett. 176 pp. Can Cleo surrender to a
passionate new love? ISBN 1-56280-159-7 11.95

COSTA BRAVA by Marta Balletbo-Coll. 144 pp. Read the book,
see the movie! ISBN 1-56280-160-0 11.95

MEETING MAGDALENE & OTHER STORIES by
Marilyn Freeman. 144 pp. Read the book, see the movie!
ISBN 1-56280-170-8 11.95

SECOND FIDDLE by Kate Kalloway. 208 pp. 2nd P.I. Cassidy James
mystery. ISBN 1-56280-161-9 11.95

LAUREL by Isabel Miller. 128 pp. By the author of the beloved
Patience and Sarah. ISBN 1-56280-146-5 10.95

LOVE OR MONEY by Jackie Calhoun. 240 pp. The romance of
real life. ISBN 1-56280-147-3 10.95

SMOKE AND MIRRORS by Pat Welch. 224 pp. 5th Helen Black
Mystery. ISBN 1-56280-143-0 10.95

DANCING IN THE DARK edited by Barbara Grier & Christine
Cassidy. 272 pp. Erotic love stories by Naiad Press authors.
ISBN 1-56280-144-9 14.95

TIME AND TIME AGAIN by Catherine Ennis. 176 pp. Passionate
love affair. ISBN 1-56280-145-7 10.95

PAXTON COURT by Diane Salvatore. 256 pp. Erotic and wickedly
funny contemporary tale about the business of learning to live
together. ISBN 1-56280-114-7 10.95

PAYBACK by Celia Cohen. 176 pp. A gripping thriller of romance, revenge and betrayal. ISBN 1-56280-084-1   10.95

THE BEACH AFFAIR by Barbara Johnson. 224 pp. Sizzling summer romance/mystery/intrigue. ISBN 1-56280-090-6   10.95

GETTING THERE by Robbi Sommers. 192 pp. Nobody does it like Robbi! ISBN 1-56280-099-X   10.95

FINAL CUT by Lisa Haddock. 208 pp. 2nd Carmen Ramirez Mystery. ISBN 1-56280-088-4   10.95

FLASHPOINT by Katherine V. Forrest. 256 pp. A Lesbian blockbuster! ISBN 1-56280-079-5   10.95

CLAIRE OF THE MOON by Nicole Conn. Audio Book — Read by Marianne Hyatt. ISBN 1-56280-113-9   13.95

FOR LOVE AND FOR LIFE: INTIMATE PORTRAITS OF LESBIAN COUPLES by Susan Johnson. 224 pp. ISBN 1-56280-091-4   14.95

DEVOTION by Mindy Kaplan. 192 pp. See the movie — read the book! ISBN 1-56280-093-0   10.95

SOMEONE TO WATCH by Jaye Maiman. 272 pp. 4th Robin Miller Mystery. ISBN 1-56280-095-7   10.95

GREENER THAN GRASS by Jennifer Fulton. 208 pp. A young woman — a stranger in her bed. ISBN 1-56280-092-2   10.95

TRAVELS WITH DIANA HUNTER by Regine Sands. Erotic lesbian romp. Audio Book (2 cassettes) ISBN 1-56280-107-4   13.95

CABIN FEVER by Carol Schmidt. 256 pp. Sizzling suspense and passion. ISBN 1-56280-089-1   10.95

THERE WILL BE NO GOODBYES by Laura DeHart Young. 192 pp. Romantic love, strength, and friendship. ISBN 1-56280-103-1   10.95

FAULTLINE by Sheila Ortiz Taylor. 144 pp. Joyous comic lesbian novel. ISBN 1-56280-108-2   9.95

OPEN HOUSE by Pat Welch. 176 pp. 4th Helen Black Mystery. ISBN 1-56280-102-3   10.95

ONCE MORE WITH FEELING by Peggy J. Herring. 240 pp. Lighthearted, loving romantic adventure. ISBN 1-56280-089-2   11.95

WHISPERS by Kris Bruyer. 176 pp. Romantic ghost story. ISBN 1-56280-082-5   10.95

PAINTED MOON by Karin Kallmaker. 224 pp. Delicious Kallmaker romance. ISBN 1-56280-075-2   11.95

THE MYSTERIOUS NAIAD edited by Katherine V. Forrest & Barbara Grier. 320 pp. Love stories by Naiad Press authors. ISBN 1-56280-074-4   14.95

DAUGHTERS OF A CORAL DAWN by Katherine V. Forrest. 240 pp. Tenth Anniversay Edition. ISBN 1-56280-104-X   11.95

BODY GUARD by Claire McNab. 208 pp. 6th Carol Ashton
Mystery.   ISBN 1-56280-073-6   11.95

SECOND GUESS by Rose Beecham. 216 pp. An Amanda
Valentine Mystery.   ISBN 1-56280-069-8   9.95

A RAGE OF MAIDENS by Lauren Wright Douglas. 240 pp.
6th Caitlin Reece Mystery.   ISBN 1-56280-068-X   10.95

TRIPLE EXPOSURE by Jackie Calhoun. 224 pp. Romantic
drama involving many characters.   ISBN 1-56280-067-1   10.95

PERSONAL ADS by Robbi Sommers. 176 pp. Sizzling short
stories.   ISBN 1-56280-059-0   11.95

CROSSWORDS by Penny Sumner. 256 pp. 2nd Victoria Cross
Mystery.   ISBN 1-56280-064-7   9.95

SWEET CHERRY WINE by Carol Schmidt. 224 pp. A novel of
suspense.   ISBN 1-56280-063-9   9.95

CERTAIN SMILES by Dorothy Tell. 160 pp. Erotic short stories.
                                            ISBN 1-56280-066-3   9.95

EDITED OUT by Lisa Haddock. 224 pp. 1st Carmen Ramirez
Mystery.   ISBN 1-56280-077-9   9.95

SMOKEY O by Celia Cohen. 176 pp. Relationships on the
playing field.   ISBN 1-56280-057-4   9.95

KATHLEEN O'DONALD by Penny Hayes. 256 pp. Rose and
Kathleen find each other and employment in 1909 NYC.
                                            ISBN 1-56280-070-1   9.95

STAYING HOME by Elisabeth Nonas. 256 pp. Molly and Alix
want a baby . . . or do they?   ISBN 1-56280-076-0   10.95

TRUE LOVE by Jennifer Fulton. 240 pp. Six lesbians searching
for love in all the "right" places.   ISBN 1-56280-035-3   11.95

THE ROMANTIC NAIAD edited by Katherine V. Forrest &
Barbara Grier. 336 pp. Love stories by Naiad Press authors.
                                            ISBN 1-56280-054-X   14.95

UNDER MY SKIN by Jaye Maiman. 336 pp. 3rd Robin Miller
Mystery.   ISBN 1-56280-049-3.   11.95

CAR POOL by Karin Kallmaker. 272pp. Lesbians on wheels
and then some!   ISBN 1-56280-048-5   11.95

NOT TELLING MOTHER: STORIES FROM A LIFE by Diane
Salvatore. 176 pp. Her 3rd novel.   ISBN 1-56280-044-2   9.95

These are just a few of the many Naiad Press titles — we are the oldest and
largest lesbian/feminist publishing company in the world. We also offer an
enormous selection of lesbian video products. Please request a complete
catalog. We offer personal service; we encourage and welcome direct mail